Valley of Death

By

Marisa L. Williams

Valley of Death
By
Marisa L. Williams

ISBN: 9798844388248
Imprint: Independently published

This book was written in
Port Charlotte, Florida

All it takes is big brutha's perspective to get things all jumbled up. Sometimes, the paranoia is justified. He tunes into things that I might look past, and when I see things through his eyes, I cannot help but take off my rose-colored glasses; in fact, he broke my rose-colored glasses.

He told me from the start that he didn't want to hear me crying, because he knew that it was inevitably going to lead to it, regardless of whatever path we chose. The tears welled up in my eyes, just like he knew they would, and he was all too happy to send the I told you so messages without saying the exact words, shoving it at me. I should have seen it coming, and part of me knew from the start that something bad was going to happen, but it was like I didn't have a choice in the matter at times.

People called him angel, but I had already seen his horns that were long enough to prove that he was not the kind of angel that was surrounded by white light. He might be an angel of the darker perspective, but others may consider him

to be more like a demon than an angel.
He's that knight of mischief that can incite
a riot at a moment's notice and dance away
carelessly into the night, not looking back.

In one prospective, my brother is a
troll, but from his prospective, he's a
prince. Is it how others see you, or how
you see yourself? I might see the best
through my rose-colored glasses, but my
brother changed my perspective quick.

I should have known by the hunting
stations conveniently located that we were
in my brother's mind, but when you travel
the wormhole so fast, it jars points of view.
Who else would have a gutting station
within steps of their back door, ready and
waiting for blood to swirl down the drain?
It slurped down the blood when I sliced
their throats, as if the drain was thirsty.

Angel hopped in to help dig a
foundation for a walkway, so they would
have an area deep enough to hide the
bodies. It's tough to slice the throat of an
old friend, but it had to be done. That's the
conundrum of the island at times, as it
turns into the Valley of Death.

12:53 a.m. July 18, 2019

Perhaps I was distracted. Slitting a childhood friend's throat can do that. Hurrying up to hide the bodies of her and her flavor of the week or lover – didn't really pause to ask how serious they were – can be a little distracting, so forgive me.

It was not glaringly obvious at first. I saw the water, so I just assumed that we were still on an island. In a metaphorical sense, we were, as in there were not a whole lot of people around, but in reality…

In the distance, I saw mountains. That's the first thing to tip me off, and it took me a while to catch on, as when fileting bodies and cleaning up their blood, I didn't really pay attention to the background so much. Then I saw who I thought was an angel, but it was just the demon, or whatever he is, that followed me, simply because I had put his cock and balls into a locked cage, with a metal tip entering down the shaft, inserting a metal rod down the piss hole, with a metal ball that goes up the poop shoot that is welded to a bar welded to the cage of the ball sack and Johnson; it looks like a car hitch that pops up the pooper and a cage for no boner.

I was still high from my dad's visions of happily ever after and white picked fences, only in a completely different setting, where it's my brother's view, my dad is not his dad, so my dad is not around in his perspective. Sure, my dad raised him, and his name was mentioned, people asked about him and things like that, but he didn't have the same blood bond I did. In his view, he almost wants me to see what it's like to not have a dad in my life.

There's not so much hatred as much as a tom cat mentality. Some tom cats will actually kill the babies of other toms. It's not like it went that far, but blood is different, which is what my Angel tried to explain to me, though I didn't get it.

While dad viewed him as a guy who would take care of me, my brother had a different perspective on the prospective. He saw it as a guy that I would be taking care of, as we were in a different location, where he wouldn't have it like he did prior. His house and posse were gone, and he wasn't the top dog; the old junk yard dog was now in charge, as we're at his house.

It's not the pretty ocean view. It's the mountains, in the middle of the sticks, with not too many people around, but there's a lake for fishing, plenty of land for hunting, and a store for what nature doesn't provide. He expected mom and I nearby, so we had houses, but Angel was simply another one of the strays I found.

In my brother's eyes, nobody would ever be good enough. Still, he liked Angel, as he had piercing blue eyes that my brother insisted were magical, and underneath his brimmed hat was a bun of hair, that when he let down, was longer than mine. Shocking locks of brown, curly hair tumbled forth from his head when my brother asked him to show me his hair.

Puffing out with the humidity, the hair took on a life of its own, turning Angel into a completely different person than from when he had his brimmed hat on. Turns out, my brother knows this cat from drum circling. Had I paid more attention, I would have remembered the conversation with my brother describing him on a number of different occasions, but I had previously tuned my brother out sometimes, hearing him ramble, but not really allowing the conversation to enter the brain, as that's what dad would do.

So, I very vaguely recall little bits of previous conversations, but it was blurry, as if he had had the conversation with dad. My father's getting older, and it's harder for him to remember things, so my memories of some the things from my time in his point of view were slowly beginning to fade away, being replaced by my brother's perspective on how things were, which was completely different, as my brother likes to play the victim card and view people as much worse than they are. In his mind, he was enslaved on the boat, but he didn't really want to be anywhere else at the same time, yet he'll still bitch.

He's still paranoid, convinced anyone and everyone is out to get him, so he's created this compound in the mountains that's nowhere as glamorous as the place I hand designed, as dad let me design it all. Dad trusted my judgement in design. Big Brutha thinks he knows everything, so it's his design, like it or not, doesn't matter what you say or how you object, as it's either that or try to traverse the mountains or not-so-massive lake.

My brother wants us to do those things, says it's good exercise. Who needs to go to the gym? Bring back dinner, too.

Go straight primitive. He makes his own weapons. The store in the middle of nowhere only has so much, just the basics.

Chip away at some flint. Start a fire. Cook and eat only what you kill or grow.

There were masses of gardens hidden throughout. Angel would laugh. "Come here, there's awesome tangerines in this spot," leading me on some wood adventure.

He almost seemed to know my brother's perspective better than me at times. Those two had this two peas in a pod thing going on, and Angel seemed to follow him around like a puppy at times. My brother expected his buddy Angel to hang out with him, just as he expected him to go home to me each night, though my brother insisted that Angel was not faithful, detailing women before me.

"I don't know how that guy can get some much pussy. You don't get it; each week, he was with a different chick. They were not all prize winners either, so I'm just saying, I don't want to hear you crying to me when the mutherfucker is slurping around the next skank; no boo-hooing.

Hindsight is twenty-twenty. Looking back, I should have seen the various signs. I should have listened and realized that we had changed into his perspective, but I hadn't caught on at that point quite yet.

I mean, it's easy for a guy to be faithful when you literally have his cock and balls caged up, locked, and you were the only one with the key; can't take out the butt plug without the key either, Boi. He's not straying too far from the key, and as much as I wasn't ready to realize that, as I wanted to believe there was a snowball's chance in hell. That's reality.

2:30 a.m. July 24, 2019

Angel was used to people responding to his whistles, but whistle as much as he wants here, and it will not yield the same. People do not wait on him hand and foot. He must consider what my brother wants.

He was in my family's territory. It's not where he rules the roost. Sure, he has a say to a point out of consideration, but the tables have turned since the island.

Grown accustomed to not having to answer to anyone, it was a switch for him. Not that he was a dick, but he could make people tremble in fear with a quick glance. There was an innate fierceness about him, that people knew to back down quickly, or to gallop with the instinct of chased prey.

Here, in the chain of command, Big Momma had him beat. She'd been losing weight on bro's real food diet, so she's not as big as she used to be. That doesn't mean that her lose of pounds made her less of an authority voice, as she's the elder and must be respected, like it or not, Angel.

There were many things that may have led up to the decision he made, but who can pinpoint his exact influence? Was it that grandma lady at the grocery store? My brother and I both happened to look over at the same time, as the shack of a party store is not very big, and we both happened to notice him put his hands on this grandma lady that was easily half a century older than me; in response, her eyes rolled back in her head, and she moaned in pleasure about a massage.

My brother and I looked each other in the eyes, as if to ask each other if we just saw what the other saw, and we both nodded an affirmation to the unspoken question simultaneously. This, needless to say, was right after I took the dick cage off. The first second his dick had freedom, he was out groping the first granny he saw.

We tried to dismiss it. Maybe he was just helping an old lady. An over-reaction?

He kept dropping hints about kids. This made my mind wonder if there was any possible way, even though my heart knew it was nowhere near the realm of hope for possibilities. It made me think he wanted a kid, up until he said, "I said that you should have a kid, not that I should be the one to give you that kid, but go have one, then you'll always have someone."

Saying something like that to someone who you know cannot have kids in a place like this is like stabbing and twisting the knife back and forth to dig in. The loaded statement also implies that he might not want to stick around for the long haul, but I didn't pick up on that at first. I was blinded by the, "oh, he's talking about kids," which makes most think long term.

It's when you start to get comfortable that you loosen the grips. In this case, it was me loosening the cage from around his cock and balls, thinking it must be safe, as we're in the middle of the mountains, with nobody around, but there's always that one fucking store that you need to go to for stuff, the last link to other humanity. For a guy, it does not matter if it's a ten or not, as it's merely a hole to put a penis into.

When brave enough to utter something, he retorts with, "better my penis smell like pussy, because it's much better than when I'm with a guy." How do you even respond to that? I was blank.

12:06 a.m. August 6, 2019

While his servants and play toys may not have made their way to the mountains, he somehow had signal for his phone to work, and he was still constantly on it. There's nothing like sitting next to someone and feeling utterly alone. Ask a question, and there's no response, as if holding a conversation with the walls.

Of course, just when you think that he's totally not paying attention, he'll randomly respond to something I said a while ago, as if totally engaged in the conversation that I thought never started. Just like I'd start to feel sorry for the guy being such a workaholic on his phone, only to peep over and see some other bitch on the screen. There comes a point and time, after so many little things add up to irritate the hell out of you, that I had to allow him to fly away: if you set him free, and he returns, then he's yours to keep.

I could've banged my head against the wall with jealousy, and that's not to say that I was overly thrilled with the situation, but my brother saw it for what it

was, and as much as he tried to warn me,
and I didn't want to accept it, I had to.
He's better off as a buddy if he's going to be
sniffing around all these other women
uncontrollably, as I didn't want to catch
their nasty diseases like
herepeghonnasyphillaids, cooties, or
whatever unheard of germy sin bacteria.
It's sort of like cutting off my nose to spite
my face, as that meant getting cut off from
a steady supply of endless money from
dad's perspective, only to turn to the
survivalist lifestyle in my brother's eyes.

My brother didn't expect an endless
stream of cash flow. He didn't trust banks.
He likes to be off-grid with no paper trail.

He didn't expect some guy to stick
around to help us, even if it was his buddy.
Times were fun when he was around, but
my brother knew that Angel was not
giving up his lifestyle for me at any time.
Bro thought it was worth bringing me to
the mountains to show me the truth of the
situation with Angel, which is that he's
there for the good times and when it
benefits him, and he could leave anytime.

Angel stuck around long enough to get the cage off of his penis and to try to make it look good, as he knew damn well that there was a chance he might need me in the future, and he didn't want to piss off my brother, as he might need him, too. Never say never in a world like this, which begs the question of whether this was the same realm as the island, or a completely different place? I've still yet to figure that.

Regardless, I didn't think that I'd miss him as much as I did, and the more I seemed to desire him, the less he seemed to even remember me, let alone care about anything that had anything to do with me. Not being able to help myself, I creeped on social media, not necessarily to stalk him, but I couldn't help it when I saw the feed. I went to wish a friend happy birthday, and instead it went to my news feed, which featured him naked with another woman.

Two days later, more pictures of him with another woman. Two days later, more pictures of him with another chick. Two days after, here's another chick that he's claiming that he's in love with now.

That's what I get for going against my brother's wishes to stay off the internet. I was glutton for punishment. I had to realize that he's not an Angel, even if his name was, as demons hurt people.

How many times had he told me that there's no such thing as a nice demon? I've yet to fully determine if that's what he is. Guess labels don't really matter if he's not sticking around for the long-haul venture.

Put the internet away. Busy the mind with big brutha's gym routine. Eat only what you catch or grow, so keep busy.

Routine numbs the mind. Go fishing. Pick vegetables and prepare food over open flames, or just chew it all raw and bloody.

Get lost in the same stuff each day. Wander the woods for hours and not see a soul. The only people that frequented the store seemed to know better than to arrive when I showed up, as they didn't want a repeat of what happened when I saw him.

Even if you have thoughts, suspicions and paranoia about your partner going behind your back with someone else, there's nothing like catching him in the heat of the moment with another woman.

Had it have been a guy, it wouldn't have mattered so much, as a guy has something that you don't have – unless you count the strap-on that is likely bigger than his dick. If a guy selects another woman over you, it's like him saying that you're not worth being faithful to, and you're simply average, that you're not special enough.

It's a special stab to the heart. I'd rather have physical pain that involved me bruising and bleeding. The inner pain that feels like a donkey kick to the chest is crippling, debilitating, and the worst kind.

Emotional pain haunts. It doesn't dissipate the way a bruise does. Lingering for years, real emo-trauma lasts a lifetime.

11:11 p.m. August 7, 2019

12:19 p.m. August 22, 2019

"Donkey punch and a dildo in the ass!" Starting slow and low, repeat the phrase over and over, raising the octave and the pacing each time. Soon feeling as if a carnival ride was going out of control on a fast forward repetition, spin in place, until that gravity pulls the stomach.

Spin until you fall down, then laugh. Brother is less amused by your shenanigans, looking like a sleeping cat that does not want to be disturbed. "That's going to be the new number one hit thar."

"It's quite catchy, isn't it?" Laugh in his face, then dance all the way back to your house. The cats are waiting for you.

Of course, you had cats. You had your inside cats, but you fed the outside cats, too, from bobcats to panthers. Your brother had always known you to have cats, so you had kittens, aka, familiars.

He had even more kinds of animals than you. He liked to keep the doors open at his house, so the chickens, goats, parrots, and even horses can waddle through at any given point and time. He felt that his house was their house, and he'd make them feel right at home – until he was ready to eat them as a meal.

Usually, he tried to save his pets for last, preferring to dine on fish and whatever random game that he caught. Eventually, the time would come for Fluffy the cow to become filet mignon and Elsie the pig to turn into bacon wrapped chops. Though he would share his food, he expected you to hunt for game, too; it wasn't time to baby lil sister for that shit.

Day in and day out, you'd forge through the forest for berries and whatever random things you could find. Often, you'd just wander and get lost, not wanting to be able to find your way home, just to be done with it all and onto a new adventure. Lonely, you tried your best to not be bored by attempting to go new ways each day.

Get lost and stumble upon a waterfall. The mountains looked almost purple up high, and the water was a sapphire blue with crystal sparkles. Catch a fish with bare hands and bring it back.

Try to find the various fruit orchards that only someone else seemed to know how to find. Even though you'd been there

before, you couldn't seem to find it again.
Each day, you'd try a different variation of
the path you remember, but each one
yields a different implausible result: how
can there be vast desert in the middle of
the woods that appears from thin air?

The more you got lost in the
mountains, the more the mountains
seemed to disappear into other landscapes.
Step into a stream, and within a few feet,
be standing on a glacier with penguins.
Reality seemed to morph in various places.

No matter how hard you tried to get
lost, you always found your way back to
familiar territory eventually. Was all this
scenery really just a glamour? Was it real?

Go take a hot shower. Rinse all the
worry out, and warm up from the hunt.
Cats watch as you towel off, and they jump
in the tub to investigate the wetness that
had been falling from towards the top.

One white cat with one gold eye and
blue eye paws into the drain. Notice gobs
of hair coming up from the drain, and
thank the cat for helping to clean, as you
pull gobs up from where the cat had
started. Looking closer, you notice the

color is darker than your hair, and you know who the long, curly hair belonged to, which made you look back with rose colored glasses, wondering what he was up to, wishing that he was back with you.

Hold the hair and will him to return. Loneliness creates the craving, as does awkwardness. When there's nobody else around, was that a glimpse of something?

Was somebody looking a little too hard at your backside? Did those eyes glance down? Are you just paranoid?

Meander out into a meadow and into the middle of a cornfield. Walk up a row, and see a figure carrying a bushel basket. Walking towards you, it took a minute to be able to make out the brimmed hat.

"I've been looking for you," he said. "I brought you some things I knew you liked." His soothing voice flowed as if nothing was wrong, and he rubbed against you like a cat: "did you miss me while I was gone?"

This shit was not a romance novel. There was no big embrace, but a smack across the face. Bitch at him for a while.

Make him feel uncomfortable. "Where's your brother? There's this big drum circle gather I need to tell him…"

Don't let him change the subject. Vent and bitch. Don't ease up of him.

Make him squirm. Double step back to the house. Grab the hitch for him.

"Don't even talk to me, until you put this damn thing back on." Shove the round, shiny metal end up his asshole. Lock his balls in a cage, and put the metal rod down the tip of his penis; lock in place.

"You were saying?" Make your voice as sweet and sugary as possible. "Continue on about this gathering spot…"

"Your brother would dig it. It looks as if you could stand to get out of the house. So, what do you say about it then?"

"How do I know you don't have a disease? How do I know you didn't knock up a whole harem? That's what I say."

"Oh… Yeah… Get it all out…"

1:11 a.m. August 22, 2019

When you're all alone, stranded in the middle of absolutely nowhere, you get lonely, and you long for what was once familiar, hoping you can find your way back to the happiness. Plaster on an artificial smile, and try to force that happiness to happen. Try to do whatever it is that you feel necessary to make it.

Think you look fat? Stop eating. If losing weight helps, do whatever possible.

Is the house not clean? Start scrubbing. Be able to lick off the toilet.

Do whatever it is you think might make your man happy. Give him awesome sex. Cook his favorite meal for him.

Thing is, it doesn't matter what you do, because if someone doesn't want to be somewhere with you, they show it eventually. Sure, they might play along, enjoy you spoiling them, because why wouldn't they? Everyone likes to be pampered when they get the chance to be.

Create an artificial reef of happiness. Swim around in it gleefully. Imagine it's real and ignore the tiny bites in your flesh.

It's like fire ants gnawing away at you. There's a little bite that pusses up for a few days, then there's just red itchiness. It's those reminders shit isn't really perfect like you want to believe wholeheartedly.

Not that it took much convincing to get your brother to go to a drum circle, but you were happy that he agreed to the voyage to get you away from the desolation. You'd lost track of how many days, months, or years had passed by you, or how many various animals waltzed into sleep in your bed. The excitement of seeing people was overwhelming to you.

It'd become even more overwhelming, as you thought that you and Angel had reached an understanding, a peacefulness. The two of you had been talking about trying to make a baby, not that you needed much convincing to have sex, but you wanted to try for the impossible. You wanted to believe you could create something in this Valley of Death.

1:51 p.m. September 6, 2019

Angel and your brother skipped off gleefully to prepare, gathering various instruments like drums and makeshift noise makers, like conch shells to blow and coconut shells to pound together like hooves stomping. As you were gathering ribbons and glow balls, you nearly got left behind by them and had to chase after them like a dog. In their excitement, they forgot all about you, so you had to try to follow the scent of their trail to the spot.

At some point, another scent was noticeable. Try to pretend that it's nothing, but you know a female's smell. Maybe she was just chasing your brother?

It feels as if you are being stabbed in the stomach, and you double over in pain. Instantly, you're trembling, shivering with chattering teeth as if you are in the cold. Turn to go back, thinking and knowing the worst is going to happen, but call yourself a fool and convince yourself that you have to soldier on to prove yourself wrong.

There's a ding on your phone. It's Angel texting you. Your heart sinks.

"I forgot to tell you that I'm meeting someone here. We had already had this planned a while ago, but you're more than welcome to come hang out with her. We had plans to eat, so you can join us there."

Your throat closes. It's hard to swallow. Even with a cage on his ballsack, he's more interested in going to meet up with some other chick and literally left you behind? He'd bring your brother, but not you, which made you think back to how close he was to your brother in the Valley.

Think back to your brother mentioning that Angel gave some of the best hugs, and remember telling him that you could not remember getting such a hug. Sure, you guys had sex, and he let you wander off to do whatever, but did Angel ever take the time to get to know what really made you tick? It seemed he knew how to get your brother excited, but he didn't bother to get you excited at all.

He merely expected you to be happy. He expected that you'd plaster a smile on your face and forgive whatever he did. He expected that it would make you feel small inside, and it did, as he was trying to dim your inner light by doing shit to make you feel bad, as he knew that'd keep you in place, keep you from trying to go anywhere or meet anyone; if he kills your self-esteem and sends you into depression, you will not have the motivation to do anything but cry.

Your brother tried to warn you that Angel hung on skanks at the drum circle, but you thought you'd be enough to quench his thirst for all that. You were wrong. When you finally made it there, all you saw was him with some brunette skank. He was trying to make her laugh and smile, while purposely ignoring your arrival, not even bothering to say hello.

Stomach pangs. Instant migraine. Hunch over, doubled over in pain, but nobody notices; in the midst of all these people, you felt utterly alone and in pain.

Each drum beat was like an ice pick to your brain. How did you become instantly afflicted, like someone had used a voodoo doll on you? It's hard to breathe.

She smiles and flips her hair, laughing and flirting with him. He flirts back, and it's like a hammer drill in your heart. Fall to the ground; nobody helps.

Everyone is too preoccupied. They're doing their own thing, following the beats of their own drumming. Too busy to care.

It's like you're in another realm, invisible to everyone, and merely able to observe. When you cry out, nobody responds. Not one person lifts their head.

Your brother is nowhere around. He seems to have went off to greener pastures. He's not around, but you thought back to what he had said about not crying when that asshole is hanging on some skank.

Try to compose yourself. Breathe deeply, even if it hurts. Slow and deep.

Stretch out. Do some yoga. Try to find that inner peace and relaxation.

Do a couple cartwheels. Bust out the glow balls. Dance alone until you hurt.

Fall to the ground again. Still, nobody notices. Try to stretch more.

Hear the bells that Angel had tied to his ankle approaching you. There's a void deep within the pit of your stomach. "I just came over to tell you that I'm leaving now."

It's like an elevator unexpectedly drops. Gravity induced loss of consciousness nearly sets in. Feel as if you are spinning, and even though he had said that you could join him, he leaves with her.

Look around, and he's gone. Feel as if you need to throw up. Cough and gag.

Everyone is gone. You're alone again. Where did everyone else go?

Wander aimlessly. Try to find a sign of life. All you can see are the stars above.

You can't even find the moon. It's just darkness with tiny specks of light. Can you even find your way back home?

2:36 p.m. September 6, 2019

11:11 pm October 21, 2019

During the mention of Adam's creation, the Bible leaves out one small detail. Were there others around? Yes, in fact, there were others – a whole breed of others.

The lowly snake in the garden is always portrayed in such an unsightly manner. The creature was cast down from out of the sky and banished to slithering on its stomach. Humans did not always rule the planet; there were dragons that soared the skies and made many tremble.

Before the whole conundrum with the Garden of Eden, many like to forget Lilith, Adam's first wife, and maybe one of the first feminists, judging by the topless hippie chicks that are known to attend the Lilith Fair. She just didn't want the burden of being a breeder apparently, and Eve donated so much to the human genetic coding, but everyone seems to forget his third wife. That's the one that inspired knowledge, a.k.a. the whole apple thing, which is more of a metaphor than some chick just eating an apple and being doomed to bleed for a week each month without dying.

Between that and celebrating Jesus being a zombie at Easter, not to mention the demon possession and prostitution, the Bible did set the stage for many a scary story. What could really be so much knowledge that would doom a race of fire breathing, high flying dragons to be doomed to become scoffed at snakes, a symbol for all that is evil? Maybe she learned the knowledge of how things would turn out?

There's crazy conspiracy theories about alien lizard people. Those are half right, as the lizard people are not alien to this planet at all. They're the original inhabitants of the planet, before people were created.

The dragons may have been doomed to slither as snakes, but there is a reason snakes are used in voodoo rituals. They hold magical powers, and part of this includes shape shifting. Much like a chameleon can pick up the hues of its environment, Adam's lineage with his third wife has the ability to portray themselves as human, but they have a different DNA than the human descendants of Eve.

Sure, Eve had God on her side. She went forth and multiplied. Humans are her descendants, and they inhabit the earth.

Descendants of dragons were doomed the crawl on their bellies, slithering around in the thick of it. Learning how to duck, dive, maneuver, be stealthy, and strike is what makes them rise into all the major positions of power. Eve's offspring can be as plentiful as they like; dragons may only lay a couple eggs in a lifetime, but the innate power drives them into all positions of leadership.

Lizard people know how to be silent and stealthy. They can wrap themselves around you in such a way that you don't even realize you're getting strangled out. They make you feel good as they kill you.

It's the carnival worker that pumps you up, exclaiming what a great job you're doing, and how you have to keep going, because you're a natural. You want to go home with that biggest teddy bear, don't you? Don't give up now, you're almost there, just keep winning your way up to the top by playing a few more rounds, until your wallet is empty.

He's that drug dealer who is always awake, no matter what the hour, who always seems to have whatever it is you're looking for, no matter how outlandish. From Brazilian roots to frogs and monkey brains, he's the one to kickstart your fun. Not saying he wouldn't kick your ass if you gave him reason, but you had that understanding, where he was more than a dealer, but a friend, a best friend…

She's that girl in the club eyeing you up, grinding on the pole, but eyes dead-set only on you. Making you think that you're special, she will lap dance your wallet empty and patiently wait for you to come back with more. Taking your phone calls and texts make you know that she must feel something, too, so you'll be back with your paycheck next week with a smile that she understands you.

It's that smooth talking Congress person that people are always excited to meet. Shake hands, smile for the camera, t2ell people what they want to hear, turn a blind eyes towards the good looking intern that keeps sniffling and picking her skin; just send her to do your guided tours and hope she can hold herself together. Promises galore, bills pass by sending the prettiest whore, but smile again for the camera.

From leading the lowest of the low to the highest of the high powered, these chameleons blend in with who they are around.

It's like when you are upset, crying. Sshhh! Someone is coming.

Choke back snot silently. Smear some on a sleeve. Gag.

Wipe tears with other sleeve. Laboriously inhale like going over a bumpy road. Lip quivers.

Back of the throat is raw like it had been sandpapered. Cottonmouth flavoring, could really use a drink of whatever is wet nearby to chase the stank breath away.

Keep trying to be slick by sucking snot silently.

Try to act like there's dust in your eyes, or maybe blame allergies. Try to rub the eyes as if they are just tired to try to mask the tears. The excess water makes the eyes glisten, but it's the opposite of glee.

That's when he's there. Though he promises not to judge, and he assures you up, down, and every way since Tuesday that he will never judge you, giving this massive grin, trying to pretend like he might actually care for a minute. Of course, anything you say will be used against you as he judges.

Drty Dck Blues

 (Why would I want out?)

I woke up this morning
To an empty bed
It made me think about
What everybody said.

I shoulda known better
I shoulda stayed away
But I jus couldn't help myself
Tempted like a buffet.

Thought if anyone
I could tame the beast
Little did I know
Love would matter least.

Got a bad case

Of dirty dick blues

Don't know if you

Heard the news.

Yeah it's a bad case

Of dirty dick blues

Should not have been so blind

To miss all the clues.

12:21 a.m. November 3, 2019

The alert on your phone dings. It's a text message from a police officer. Your heart rate quickens.

Anger boils inside. "Fuck da Police" is like a soundtrack in your brain. The pit of your stomach churns.

He's asking you out to lunch, though when you told him your normal work schedule, it must not have registered, unless he was going through the motions of asking, knowing that you were not available. It's his lame attempt to cover his tracks with the ye olde "can't say I didn't ask" trick. This type of behavior would not seem as bad had you not found out about his Childress choices, such as dating his ex's best friend, just to piss off his ex and be spiteful, which is not the sort of game that you want to waste life on.

The whole thing started from a misunderstanding the first time he asked you out. You typed a response, but the message never sent, leading you to think he was ignoring you, while he thought you were ignoring him. He went so far as to say something to a mutual friend, but you wondered why he had to cry to his friend like a bitch, as opposed to simply calling you on the phone like a man; fuck texting.

Six months later, when you decide to break the ice, you see your message was never sent and try to apologize. Ask him out to a concert you have to cover. He says he's interested a week in advance, but you never hear back from him until you text on the night if the show to see if he's really going or not.

Some lame excuse is muttered, with no real explanation til the day after, as if an after thought, unless he needed that much time to think of some story that sounded believable enough to pass as an excuse. It's all about anxiety. Let bygones be bygones, as there's a rumor his kid was ran over by a drunk driver in front of him, and since you had previously ghosted him when you were too bullheaded to simply double check to make sure your message was received, you opt to let this one slide as a Mulligan.

He generically says you two should go out, which leads to you planning a second date attempt by inviting him to a haunted house. He says he's game, so you set the date and time, only to never hear boo back from him until the day after it ended, and only since you initiated it. It's pulling the nearly identical behavior a second time in a row that got under your skin so bad.

Text him back that you're working. You know he already knows that. "While I appreciate the offer, I have a cat to cuddle and a dildo for the rest, so I'm good."

12:51 am November 3, 2019

1:03 a.m. November 4, 2019

There's nothing like rejection to make a man want you more. Just when you're at witt's end, you'll figure throwing in the towel is easiest, that's when you won't be able to avoid admitting that there is some little twinkle of decency, as he will try to make honor

8:12 p.m. November 4, 2019

Once again, I've been bad. I pissed everyone off without even trying. Had I been trying, they really would not have liked me, but the fact of the matter is that I had the best of intentions with it all.

It's like he pulled something out of me. Something had been sleeping dormantly under the façade of being this perfectly normal person, doing boring, everyday shit. Call it an alter ego if you will.

I'm not going to say that I was completely innocent when I was younger. The first time I met him, I was getting body painted from head to toe as a leopard, as my ex-boyfriend was a body painter. This guy was working on Lazy Way, a friend of my now ex-boyfriend, who nodded over at him and said, "oh, that guy's cool – he's gay, so you don't have to worry about anything," before I proceeded to strip to only a leopard-print g-string that was a see-through mesh, allowing my tattoos to show underneath.

I mean, given that is how I met the guy nearly 20 years ago, can he really be surprised if my tits jiggle if I wear a corset? I mean, A-cup titties might not have an issue, but anyone with double-dees should be expected to have some spillage. Sure, boobies jiggle, but it's not an intentional thing.

It's just the motion in the ocean. Like any fat roll, there can be jiggles. It's almost wave-like.

The only reason I went out and bought a corset, as in intentionally spent money, was because other girls were wearing them. The whole theme was steampunk, so girls planned on corsets with mullet skirts – short in the front and long in the back. They also talked about those mini-top hats.

"Steampunk is basically pirate, so if it'd look good for a pirate, it'd probably look good for steampunk," I was told. I'm thinking lusty, busty wenches, since girls are talking corsets. I'll admit, there was a little wardrobe malfunction, because what do you expect when you're ordering straight from China and have to guess the

size, causing me to order the biggest,
which may have been a little too big?

All the pieces of the outfit cost me a
few hundred, which I did not go out and
spend with ill intentions in my heart; I can
assure you of that much. One usually good
thing about gaining weight is that tits get
bigger, but apparently, everyone has a
limit on how much is too much of a good
thing. Personally, I thought it was my dad
who didn't know how to tie a corset right,
and I figured one of the girls would know
how to do a better job at tying it up, but it
wasn't as simple as that as it turned out.

Who woulda thought that made in
China was not the same as quality made
by hand with care? Guess those Chinese
don't have too many DD's. I probably
should have brought another top on
standby, because I did find out that the
overcoat was not big enough to cover the
titties either.

That was another quality straight
from China purchase where I didn't know
what size was really what, so I ordered
smaller than the other, but this was a tad
too small, as I couldn't button the breast.

Does it count that I paid good money for it,
but didn't have time to ship it back to
China to exchange it? I mean, I did plan
on having something to cover up with, and
I did wear it, but I couldn't button it, and
that damned air conditioning was not
working, so I had to take it back off once I
was sweating so bad.

9:51 p.m. November 4, 2019

As much as you want to tell him to fuck off, there's times when you know that having a cop on your team is a good thing, such as when unexpected company arrives and tries to claim your home as their own. That's when you need to be able to phone a cop to convince people to leave. Sometimes, it's hard to be able to put a foot down, as this niceness is engrained into the blood with 500 chances.

Wanting to give the benefit of the doubt, hoping the best of people, it sets the stage to be let down. Hope for change, believe in it likc a magical fairy, but don't be surprised when it's the same old shit. There's convincing stories that make you want to think otherwise, but alas, should have known.

Just when you want to throw in the towel, there might be that momentary glimmer, a faint sparkle that is enough to convince you to doubt your snap judgments. There's a flash of something worthwhile that allows you to hold on, but time shows the truth. Time will tell if a cop is required or not.

Let's keep him in the back pocket, just in case of emergency, in case shit goes down in epic proportion, which is entirely possible when there's multiple guys trying to lay claim on one house that is owned by one chick, which means only one pussy hole to fill with cock. Surely, there's the fantasy that you could be on the bed, legs spread, while one is bare and about to mount you, when the other bursts out the closet like the Kool-aid man ready to fuck that guy in the ass, but would they play nice together?

It's funny how you can be all depressed and lonely, but when you buy a house, all kinds of burners show up out of the woodwork, all excited to try to lay claim on your hole and home. Catch them in bullshit lies and excuses for everything. It's all a matter of how much you put up with, until you call the cop friend.

Just tell him to park the cruiser in the driveway. That's a clear message to those who want to pop by. Some might be too stupid to get it, but a night stick might convince them or a taser to widen eyes.

11:22 a.m. November 7, 2019

3:08 a.m. November 8, 2019

Back in the day, superheroes often change in telephone booths. Now the telephone booths are not as common as they were once before, it seems that all one needs is a refrigerator box. Pop it up in a moments notice, and all you need is one little whore, and the rest is all about making some quick cash.

For years, he went traveling around, holding up a piece of cardboard. Had he known then what he knows now, all he needed was to unfold the cardboard box. That could serve as shelter and the workplace on the go at any street corner in the world, like a universal beacon of hope from the corner.

For some, it is the thrill of the surprise. A quarter for a thrust, but they do not know what it is that they are thrusting into. It could be a hand, and moist mouth, or a dirty asshole that is more than a little blown out.

Some start slow with just one little hole. Eventually though, greed gets the best of people. Poke A hole in each side of the refrigerator box, so that way you can serve front to back, along with side to side.

Maximize the potential. Work your way up from Vaseline to poly grip. Be the best you can be.

With enough due diligence and hard work, you might even be lucky enough to manage a Gloryhole. These pop-up portable glory holes could be the Surd of them are $10 million business, and you could be the regional manager of your own series of Gloryhole workers. Got to have inspiration and aspirations.

Wave goodbye to your spouse out the kitchen window, then scamper like your asshole is on fire, and raise for the nearest refrigerator box. Venture out the door on your mission, and find a cozy corner to set up shut up. Next thing you know, there is a line for miles and miles, as far as the eye can see.

Try to break some world records on how many can be serviced at your Gloryhole. Don't even do it for the fame or the money. Do it because you love to service people that much, and spread it wide.

Some people have a beacon for the Gloryhole. It is like a built-in antenna, or like a GPS, then alerts them to the nearest Gloryhole. Someone jumped up in a panic, eager at the idea of a nearby gloryhole, but a tad skeptical: "if there was a Gloryhole around here, I , of all people, would surely know about it!"

3:22 a.m. November 8, 2019

2:05 a.m. November 11, 2019

The one proclaiming to everyone on the loudspeaker about his built-in GPS for glory holes, just happens to be the guy that has your heart at the moment. Of course, you were nearly suicidal, not understanding why he wanted a whore around with 1 million other women. The truth of the matter might be the fact that he was taking in the ass but his grandfather, he has disrespect for women, he has very feminine tendencies, and you never know if he might've taken ass a few too many to even pretend to be straight.

It's like he's getting revenge against his mother by juggling a bunch of different women like his father did. He knows that's what hurt his mother the most growing up, so he does it just out of sheer Rebellion. People always tend to want the ones that push them away the most, as it creates the forbidden fruit taboo, making it all that more desirable, because you know you can't really get it.

You cannot even say that the guy lied, for he was straight up about the fact that he whored around with a multitude of women, as people were always refer to one of his girlfriends, plural. He like to hide in that hippie idea of one love, trying to blow smoke up women's asses that they don't have to be monogamous, but it's really him being a health risk in spreading disease without a condom. When guys choose quantity over quality, there's a major reason why they have walls around their heart and don't want women to get too close to them, and it's easier said than done to break down the walls.

Some men like a large quantity of women, as it makes them feel better about themselves. They justify their own self-worth based on how many women they can get with. They think that if women desire them, than that justifies their manliness, and maybe society is partially to blame for that mentality.

There is certainly a number of women who think that they are being liberal by being slutty.   They try to convince themselves that it's been a man's world for so long, that they should also be able to enjoy being a honeybee. They are just as interested in different actors, but they failed to understand that those scenarios create drama that one's up on Jerry Springer show was trying to figure out who the baby daddy is, combined with lines of guys who are eager to deny that they had anything to do with the situation, easily forgetting that it takes two to do the horizontal mambo In heated passion .

When something was woken up from inside me, I made this shift from the logic and reason it says no, be faithfully monogamous, so the other side of the coin that said were sick of living in a man's world. It wasn't so much of my mentality, so much of the mentality of the penis radar. Once a man gets a notion that there is another penis in the picture, then suddenly penises show up from out of the woodworks.

All it takes is a simple post on social media with an unknown male, and the next thing you know, there are penises popping out of the woodwork's like you haven't even seen. Forget about that depression and loneliness, forget about those suicidal thoughts of thinking you'll die alone, because they'll be too many penises to handle. You'll be better in an away with a broom wondering how they all came out at once, and where the hell were they for the years when you were crying in your beer about being sad and lonely Lake some degenerate country western song that nobody wants to hear alone.

It's that polar opposite feeling from feeling completely abandoned to the point that you feel life isn't even worth living, add to being pushed front and center in to the front of the spotlight. Suddenly, everyone is checking you out, judging you, pointing out your flaws and your unique skills. From being sad lonely, to having your pic of many, it's overwhelming to not know which penis to go to.

There will be a penis is breaking down your door. Before you know it, there will be a penis in your bed, and you won't even realize how the hell it got there. It will be moving into your house, moving clothes in your closet, and taking over half of your bathroom area, claiming stage in your home land turf.

That's the weird way that last works. One minute you were lusting over something you can't have, then the next minute there are other is the scene over you that can't have you. That's the irony of life.

2:22 a.m. November 11, 2019

2:10 a.m. November 12, 2019

Even the caterpillar hast to hide away, spinning a wall around itself, keeping everyone out. There's work that has to be put in, things that have to be changed, in order to have a transformation. When the butterfly emerges, it's not looking for a gold star in the forehead, it's merely moving on with its life.

Not everyone is into caterpillars, as some look really scary with spikes and bumps and funky colors. There's a lot more people who like to watch the majestic butterflies flying around, or floating around like angels or fairies. People understand that it takes a character pillar to become a butterfly, but not everyone appreciates the butterfly in its caterpillar stage, before it develops gracious, elegant wings.

2:22 a.m. November 12, 2019

1:31 a.m. November 13, 2019

The darkness closed in around, like a suffocating abyss of nothingness and nobody. Attempting to feel around, the knee clunks into something solid, wooden: a table. Feeling around blindly, the hand feels something small and metallic; picking it up, it's heavier than copper; wonder what it could be.

The object in the pocket. With the other hand, feel around until another object is touched. Feel of words the slender pull the the mind identifies as a lamp when a pole switch is found; pull it to have light blind.

Eyes adjust to a figure sitting silently staring. He is wearing a mask with a long nose in the style of the doctors dealing with pockets full of posies during times of Black Death. "What's in your pocket?"

Try to stammer a response, but words fail to form. Give up and reach into the pocket, pulling out a one ounce gold bar that's inscribed with "join us" on one side and "The Aristocrats" on the other side.

"Well? What do you say? Are you ready?"

Eye up the masked person. Even after hearing the voice, you could not tell if it was a woman or a man sitting before you. Arch an eyebrow questioningly and inquire, "and who are you exactly now?"

"I'm merely the talent's manager; I'm a scout. Always on the hunt for new talent, but this show is one for the books, not to be mussed, as it's a family affair and invitation only to see a show at all. They practice ways of past aristocratic society with a bit of a modern twist you have to see to appreciate."

Lightly toss the coin. It lands on the "join us" side. "This real gold?"

"But of course. What would you expect? Kill trees with a paper trail?"

Chuckle at the innovation. "Any other options? Anything to know?"

"Only death. Go or die. Two options."

Try not to look phased by the masked guy's lame attempt at humor. "Let's go see this show then. Is it guaranteed to be something worth dying for, or more lame-o hogwash on rye but all raw and nasty?"

"It is a show worth seeing. There are three generations on stage. It's a family affair."

The masked figure offers an elbow, escorting you through a thick fog to a horse drawn carriage. Opening the carriage door, a hand is offered to help you step inside. Black lambskin leather seats, a wet bar with cigars, and a glass case with rhinestone dildos, fur handcuffs, and a variety of fur whips were inside.

Reach to open the case, and a midget pops out from underneath the seat. "Here. Let me help with that."

A diamond covered dildo is selected and turned on. With the other hand, the midget has already unbuttoned and then zip the pants. The second but the pants were down, you didn't even remember feeling the impact, but you just heard the midget proudly recite, "donkey punch and a dildo at once."

The room got dark. Wake up to a horse tailed butt plug in your ass. You have blinders on. Someone gently strokes your head, "whoa there big fella, would you say you're as hungry as a horse right now?"

Try to talk, but there's a bit in your mouth. Nod your head up and down like Mr. Ed. Nostrils flare.

The bit is taken out of your mouth. A feed bag is put over your head, it's not some old grains alone though; there's some ground up meat that has a nice blend of spice without being fiery on the ass.

As you munch, a spotlight breaks darkness. An old woman explains that the best dancer was asked to do the lotus dance, which meant binding the feet to be like hooves. As she explains, a young man bursts in another spotlight dancing around his grandmother, roses shower the stage, and he bows at her feet.

Grandfather appears with a rope and a hammer. He sets the young dancer in a comfortable chaise lounge chair that is red velvet and begins hammering his toes underneath his feet. Bones crack.

Once the bones are broken, grandma lovingly binds the feet in the Japanese tradition, while grandpa dunks his balls into his grandson's eagerly open mouth, the proceeds to fountain a stream of piss. The father stalks in from the darkness, holding metal horse shoes, long nails, and a hammer. Pulling up grandma's night gown, he bends her over, fucking her in the ass, while at the same time hammering long nails into his son's feet, permanently affixing metal horse shoes into his already broken feet.

They put the son naked into a pasture, where he gets mounted by a real stallion. The horse's cock is too big to enter the grandson, though a variety of tries are attempted, so he has to manually jerk off the huge horse cock, while licking it up and down, trying to get as much saliva onto the cock as possible. It glistens with dripping drool, so the grandson is able to lessen the friction, when his sister comes out.

Now that he's primed the well, she tries to slide the horse's cock inside her, while her brother continues to slurp and rub the cock, gliding it into his his sister the best he can, so when the horse finally cus, he sprays all over her orifices and her body, showering her in horse semen, while her brother tries to slurp. As the horse finishes, mom guides the animal off stage, while the brother first starts licking the semen off his sister's orifices, then slowly starts to insert his head inside of her widened, semen dripping vagina. He gets to his eyebrows when grandma fists him in the ass as a helping hand, then he's a puppet.

Meanwhile, grandma is having her anal ring tongued by her daughter, who is getting fucked by grandpa in the ass, until she shits all over his cock with a brown rain that doesn't seem to stop him at all. Once he cums, he gathers the mix of shit and semen, and handfuls it into his grandson's mouth, before pulling him by the ear to the slaughterhouse: "there's a big calling for horse meat in the black market here." He takes a couple meat hooks, drives them through his grandson's back and hoists him to dangle from the two hooks in his back, which causes the skin to pull from the muscles of the back, puckering gathers.

Other bodies are on hooks, too, but they're all missing various body parts and have long been dead. Mom slices strips of flesh off one body's buttocks and puts it into a frying pan to sauté with butter. The hooded figure startles you by asking, " I pray that you found your meal satisfactory this evening…"

3:13 a.m. November 13, 2019

1:03 a.m. November 14, 2019

The masked figure starts to take off your feed bag. Shoot up a hand to stop him. "Nothing wrong with a little cannibalism amongst friends," slurp up the last bite, then allow him to remove it from your head.

Bite the bit eagerly. Flick your horse tail by squeezing your cheeks. Give a lil whinny and a wink.

They like the way you think. You're not afraid to have the flesh of your genitalia stabbed repeatedly by needles, telling people to think of a genital piercing like a bee sting with momentary pain. Be a freak.

That's why you were given an invitation. The gold bar was in your pocket no less. They tried to shock.

You're not really phased. It takes a lot more than some three generational incest, some horse fucking, and a dude nailing lotus feet to phase you. There's too much stimulation for things to be shocking.

Incest happens all the time. Many would be jealous of the money they were making off the bit, as most incestuous situations are not necessarily turning a profit, but power to the underground marketing.

"We need to team the cooks up with the snuff video makers." Crack a smile. Nod at the mask.

The mask was turned in your direction. You couldn't tell if the person under the mask was amused or not, but the eye holes faced your direction. You were used to shenanigans like M.O.M.'s Ball in New Orleans – the Misfits of Mayhem have parties with Mardi Gras floats of years past and costumes.

Masks were not scary or intimidating for you, as you often liked to hide under a mask or in another skin. You were known for picking up and leaving on a whim, going across the globe, starting fresh again. Each time you moved, it was like a roll of the dice who you would meet or what you'd get into in a new city.

Create any type of mask, from sweet to scary, to lure people in or scare them away. People wear masks everyday. Some masks are simply more visible than others; some blend so naturally, one wouldn't know.

1:31 a.m. November 14, 2019

5:17 p.m. November 16, 2019

When someone is into incest, they were a mess but everything is perfectly normal. Sometimes, they may seem like the "Leave it to Beaver" family. It's not like people get tattoos that advertise that they fucked their family members; sure, maybe someone out there has, but that's not how people can tell.

When animals and breed, they call them purebred. Royals he had inbred for centuries. That's how you stay rich, by keeping everything in the family, so no one else can ever lay claim to money or power.

There's more people on the planet that have had an experience of incest than people realize. It's really not that shocking if there's a lot of people who have experienced it. It's that people don't advertise it.

It's not the conversation that people have around the school lunch table. They don't compare notes on dad, brother and uncle to friends, unless the friends are doing them, too. That's a whole nother level.

With time, there may be signs of trauma, but sometimes there's not. Some people might internalize everything, have problems with relationships, but there's no standard certain set way to act. Others may have absolutely no signs at all whatsoever, and just go about life to their degree of normal: daily grind...

5:31 p.m. November 16, 2019

12:34 a.m. November 18, 2019

Piercings have become part of the daily grind. Even infants get their ears pierced now and teenagers regularly get whatever piercings they want. Do you have needle poke flash is not all that shocking.

Tattoos and piercings have become more common pleas. They're not just for circus freaks. Everyone from CEOs to movie stars and every day people with frequent bars have tattoos and piercings. It's not like it's serving the purpose like the Vikings, where it was so shocking it would scare the enemies; instead, it has become commercialized, the things to do to fit in, something to make you unique.

The needle going into the flesh is like a bee sting. Blink and you will miss it. It's quick, hot pain.

12:42 a.m. November 18, 2109

9:46 p.m. November 18, 2019

It's like being in utter darkness. Lack of light envelops you. It nearly destroys you.

Hibernate. Sleep so long you forget you're asleep. It's not time for the grave though.

Part of you didn't plan on waking up ever again. Most of you didn't want to wake up at all. There's always that sappy little cheerleader part of you that gets everything else going, want to or not.

It's so easy to get used to the daily grind, whatever that may be. Get dropped off on a different planet, in a completely different setting, and eventually, there will be a routine to learn and get used to. No matter how rewarding, insulting, demeaning, unholy, satisfying, or whatever, get used to it.

Put on the blinders. Go on autopilot. Do your thing.

Whatever it is that your thing may be, try to do it well. It becomes second nature; even if it wasn't when you first started, it becomes that way with time. Do it in your sleep, as they say, and if you do enough of the same thing everyday, it's as if your mind goes to sleep, as it is no longer stimulated.

Get lost in the daily abyss. It takes a jolt to shock you awake. Something has to happen.

It's like a chain reaction. One thing leads to another. But it's instant like chemical reactions.

Something happens to jolt you awake. It's like an electric shock. Eyes open wide.

The funny thing is, looking back, you cannot pinpoint what exact thing caused the awakening. Was it getting dressed into an outfit that was a little too similar to your past, and was it that same outfit that caused to much of a raucous? That outfit definitely caused eyes to widen when they saw you in it.

It's not your fault for having one of those bodies that pulls off outfits that other people can't. It's called having curves. Sorry stick figure models, but you can't pull off the curves even if you tried.

Natural jiggles and is soft to the touch. It's called fat. It's what boobs and asses are made of.

Natural is cushiony. People can sink into it. That's what makes it so comfortable.

Bones are not cozy. They poke into skin. Sorry skinny people.

Everyone likes to forget that thick girls can be attractive. Media is so busy making sure that only skinny is in style, but they forget that comfort factor when cuddling. Curvy women are made to feel bad about themselves, being told they need to starve on a diet and work out until they pass out or they suck.

You can feel bad about yourself, feeling as if you're the worst person on the planet, and there's always someone who has it worse than you. You can feel as ugly as sin. Someone will still fuck you.

When you're isolated from the rest of the world, cut off from the main stream of society, you don't think you're anything special. Whenever a new person comes around a group of people, they are fresh meat in every way, shape, and form. People like to pounce on what's new and therefore exciting.

The boys has suggested the drum circle, and when you've been away from people so long, it's odd adjusting. At first, you saw the people and sat back, but then all the people disappeared. It's like you were in utter darkness, like the floor dropped out from beneath you, and you were floating in void.

Gravity did not desert you, as you could feel it pulling down on your heavily. The music went away, along with the people and the surroundings. It was simply you in the dark feeling confused.

Just because you couldn't see anyone did not mean that they couldn't see you. All eyes were on you from the moment you were a speck on the horizon, because you were new and therefore exciting. You didn't take in any names, faces, or details, before you felt abandoned and alone in the dark abyss.

Though you had been about to cry from being alone and so confused by why you had been summoned there in the first place, you felt a head nuzzle up to your shoulder. A man's voice whispered in your ear, "I have long, dark hair and blue eyes, too. Sorry to say, but I would adore you more…"

The touch of another human was startling enough, but the words were not what you were expecting. Turn, but you only see the top of his head. Note the long, baby doll ringlets, a tad greasy.

"Who are you?" No matter how you try, you cannot see all of him. "How do you know me?"

"I'm Adam, and I'm not going to lie. I have a past. I have an ex named Eve."

"Most people have ex's, don't they? Guess people probably would've referred to you as a pretty Biblical couple, huh? I can only imagine you heard that more than a bit with those names."

"We were the Biblical couple actually." Adam cleared his throat. "You heard of me?"

"That's funny." You roll your eyes. He is not laughing.

"My reputation proceeds me once again." His voice was thick with more annoyance than sarcasm. "Most people think we only lived 900 years, but we were only together for 900 years."

He sighed. He obviously had explained this more than once. He knew you were confused.

"Why do people forget that Eve and I both died on a number of occasions? We were the first immortals, as we just kept being reborn, which is how we had so many children over the millennium. We were the first to learn by trial and error, before it was cool, dying from things like drowning.

"That's how we learned water can kill you, as it killed us. We burned, fell to our deaths and died almost every way imaginable, and we continue to die in new and old ways each time that we die. Eve was made from my rib, so she's a part of me, just like me, but we got sick of each other after a while."

Arch an eyebrow at him, even though he can't see it, as his head is settled on your shoulder. He can sense that you don't believe him, as so many others had not over the years. "Look, you try being with the same person in and out, day after day, century after century, and it gets old after a while.

"They say if you start to feel jaded, like you've done everything, do all those things again with someone who has never done them before, so you can see what it feels like to experience those things through their eyes. After a while, with Eve, it was like that. We both needed to try the same old boring stuff again with new people who had never done what we had, so we could feel a little more alive."

"So," you hesitated, trying to find the right words, "let's say I buy into what you're saying. That still doesn't explain how you know about me or who you might be referring to when you said more. Are you saying that since you've done so much, you've gotten these psychic friends' abilities or something?"

"Please," he snarked, "it doesn't take a psychic to know the one you came here with. I'm not going to say his name, because that will surely summon him here to our dark little corner, but let's just say I know your friend whose name starts with an 's.' You do know his real name though, right?"

"Um…" your mind came up blank. With all the fantasy from your dad's dream wedding, all the talk of him being your brother's buddy, why didn't you know his name that starts with that letter? "Are you sure that you and I are thinking of the same person, because I'm trying to think with that letter…"

"Uh, if you don't know, I'm not going to be saying it right now. Sorry. Let's say that's his name."

Notice his head move as your body reacts to the laughter, causing a wave of motion that rocks his head as comfortingly as a baby in a cradle. His eyes glance up at you; those sky blue eyes become visible, a lighter blue than the man he was referring to, whose were so dark, they were nearly navy.

"I can't believe he's got you caught up in whatever fantasy, and he still hasn't even uttered his real name, which I can't blame him, as his name has a power over him different from you and I anyhow. There's rules for all the creatures in the universe, and Honey, there's some quack jobs you haven't met. I'm not going to ruin the surprise, or lack thereof, by babbling about that, but I will try to warn you.

"Notice I say try, as I already know it's more likely that you'll make the wrong decision and go for the guy who pushes you away, as people always want what they can't have. Go after the bad boy type with the defensive walls that won't even tell you his real name. What do you expect from Lust?"

"His name is not Lust," you smirk. He's not laughing though. He shakes his head.

"You've heard of the sin lust? That guy's the one who promotes it, so it's real easy for girls to fall head over heels in love with the guy, but he's not the real warm and fuzzy type to reciprocate it back. His ego depends on men and women going after him; his self-worth is created by others."

There was basically an orgy in his house on more than one occasion. Usually daily. He wasn't the warm and fuzzy, but you were the one he wanted in his bed over all the others around his house.

11:11 p.m. November 18, 2019

Computer just now reset itself back for daylight savings (better late than never).

10:53 p.m. November 18, 2019

You were never known as being overly affectionate in public, so standoffishness is normal. He was affectionate when he wanted to be, on his own terms, and you had plenty of sex, even marriage. The cold ways didn't start until there was a change in scenery, nobody else around, and without the constant orgy around to take in, his eyes wandered to whoever he could find, even a simple clerk.

Keeping his dick under lock and key didn't even work. He longed to feel that longing. He had a need to be constantly desired, and Adam's words started to make a little too much sense somehow.

"Think of the devil, and he appears." Adam's voice was thick with sarcasm. "Hello, Samael."

The angel did not look up from underneath his brimmed hat. "Sup, Adam?" Though he mumbled to Adam, he did not stop staring at you, and Adam refused to lift his head from your shoulder.

Shift underneath Adam's weight, which seemed to weigh ten-fold. The drumming seemed to kick back in from being lost in the background, and the people of the drum circle started coming into focus. Many tried to pretend to be lost in their drumming, but you felt their peering eyes upon you.

"How did we get married, without me knowing that name?" Samael ignored your question. He just played a drum and was watching you interact with Adam as if he was watching a television show.

"Free love, Mon," a Jamaican voice sang out. "Why can't we have love the free way; why do we feel the need to be handcuffed to monogamous beliefs? We should be free to love who we want."

That was not really the message you felt like hearing. "I might have some guy leaning up against me right now, but I haven't kissed him, haven't fucked him. That's how I am, but that's not really you."

Nod up to Samael. He nods a no back. He's not trying to deny who or how he is.

"Therein lies the predicament," you sigh. "I'm not like you. I don't want the town bicycle."

He shot you a look that said you knew damn well that he didn't want the used bike either. Not saying he wouldn't hop on one if he needed a ride, but he was spoiled enough to be selective usually. Of course, his standards and yours varied greatly, as evidenced by lovers both of you had in the past.

Judging by ex's, some might say you had the lower standards in some abusive cases. Numbers he had you over the past few years, but there were years in the past where you were not so innocent. It takes one to know one mentality perhaps attracted you two to be together without trying to hide it.

Was there even a first date? You just showed up. It was on.

There was no romantic wooing. Samael sees Adam leaning on you, whispering in your ear, but he doesn't stick around to hear the conversation. He ventures off around the drum circle but watches.

He found some pretty young thing to keep his interest. Adam scoffs, "even with you right here, he can't control himself around other women. I can feel your body tense to know it bothers you."

You hadn't even realized your muscles had tensed up. It feels like knots tied deep within a variety of muscles. It bothered but fascinated you that Adam was in tuned enough to pick up on this.

It's not that you were bothered that Adam noticed. It was moreso you were bothered that Samael didn't seem to notice or care. A stranger can pick up on more than Samael has been able to.

You liked the idea of somebody new looking at you, and you liked the feel of another's skin against your own, but you felt as if his body was made of lead, as he added so much pressure. The weight of his body was too much, and it made you shift uncomfortably, but he didn't adjust at all. Try to wiggle yourself into as comfortable of a body pillow position as you could make yourself for his weight.

"All I can do is warn you. I can't make you listen. I can't make you believe me."

11:39 p.m. November 18, 2019

11:45 p.m. November 19, 2019

You knew what Adam said made sense, and you knew that you should head his warning. At the same time, you felt this unrelenting loyalty that didn't make you want to stray too far from him at all. In fact, it bothered you when he strayed off, and even a stranger could pick up on details of the tension.

Part of you was not entirely trusting of Adam. What guy just comes up and

leans on a chick? He could be a test for all
you knew, as the two of them shared some
characteristics, so you were paranoid.

He intrigued at the same time. More
conversation reveals similarities. Moth to
a flame.

The decision came down to the
birthday. That probably sounds so bad to
say it like that. When he revealed that his
birthday was on the same day as a couple
other people who had previously come into
your life – both with deep connections, but
both who eventually did you dirty in
harmful, mean ways – you mentally
decided to pass on even opening that door
a whole lot further, just to be safe.

Prove him right. Try to hold onto
someone who want to go. Guess what
happens?

Someone who is determined to leave
is going to leave. There's no ifs, ands, or
buts about it. The more that you try to
hold onto Samael, the further it sends him
away from you, but it's when he leaves
that others show up on the step looking for
you, as if they can smell the fresh meat on
market.

It's only after he's gone that you wish you would have listened to Adam. You should have just left with him, just to see what happened. There's so many questions that would randomly pop up in your brain, and you would want to kick yourself, wondering why you didn't think of it when he was there, standing right in front of you, and you didn't like that the ghost of him was rattling in your head.

Smack in the middle of nowhere, a visitor shows up on your door. Phone calls start coming in from people you'd forgotten about, wondering if they can come and see you. People you hadn't thought about since before you'd gone to the island, people from seemingly another life ago, blew up your phone like you hadn't missed a beat, wondering when they could come by and say howdy.

Was there a memo sent out to any penis that you've ever touched before? Was there some sort of mental connection to all of them saying that there's an opening at your hole that needs to be filled? The worst part was not really feeling attracted to any of them, as you couldn't get off the Samael kick.

Be like a plant. Turn inward.
Provide your own satisfaction.

12:07 a.m. November 20, 2019

1:21 a.m. November 20, 2019

"I am glad we can have these conversations. Most people cannot go there, refuse to go there, but I am glad we do not have such boundaries and restrictions. Unfortunately, I think there's someone at my door that I must attend to, so as much as I hate to run away from such an open conversation..."

That's when you went too far. The gotta go. Symphony's playing; wind it up.

Those words came from a guy who is in a picture with his evil grin as he placed a padlock on your vagina. It's not the typical Mr. Rogers' Neighborhood poster on the street, granted, but if you can't talk about period hemorrhage and popping cysts with someone who has proof of padlocking your vagina, who could you share the details with whether they liked it or not; why do you have to be sexy to them?

As others are crying that they're cold, bundled up in sweaters, you're wearing a thin, white t-shirt and are dripping sweat.

They say you look pale. Try to be tough by
letting the frustrations vent

1:40 a.m. November 20, 2019

1:32 a.m. November 21, 2019

It's when you want to be left alone that everyone wants to bug you. Not that you were irritated, but it's easy to be comfortable in the daily grind, then have it shaken up by unexpected happenings. Especially when that includes people showing up with their own habits, expecting you to change.

Just because people want you does not mean that you want them back. Just because you used to want someone doesn't mean that you want them now. People and feelings change with time.

No matter how intimate you used to be with someone, when you spend enough time away from that person, it's easy to be especially irritated by the bad habits that made you mad before. People can change, they can unlearn bad habits, but when those habits become second nature, it's hard to break. It's like people who mindlessly have a cigarette after eating, then when they quit, they miss the ritual.

When Samael is gone, you miss the daily habits – at least, some of them. You didn't really miss him pounding away on his phone, especially when you saw him looking at or talking to other women. You didn't miss feeling so alone when you were there next to him, as if you didn't register on the radar.

The jealousy bits were not something that you missed either. Who misses feeling as if they don't matter? When you talked, but it didn't really ever register in his mind, so it didn't really count.

It'd be a lie to say that you did not miss the sex, as that was something rather spectacular most of the time, not always the same old missionary position, though he did like doggy a little too much. That's the pose to depersonalize sex, where you don't have to be reminded of the face. Knowing that made the position bothersome in that regards, but when it's hitting the spot, what can you really say?

What bothered you was knowing that the two of you had some sort of a connection, but it wasn't enough to prevent him from being able to walk away, no matter what you had to say about it. It's like your opinion, your feelings, did not really matter in his equation, only when it was convenient for him. Sure, he knew how to say the love word and smooth talk when he wanted, but he didn't always feel the need to do so, more thinking that the women folk where moreso here to slave for the men.

That's not really something you were down for, as you were not raised like Mary Homemaker. People never expected you to be barefoot and pregnant in a kitchen, so why want to do that now? Keeping busy was more part of your nature than you realized, and you were not one to sit back and be told what to do complacently, but you did know some people in the right places, who gave you tips.

1:54 a.m. November 21, 2019

1:52 a.m. November 22, 2019

Hot and cold sweats cause a dripping forehead and goosebumps on the skin. Smile with a brave face. Try to act as if everything is okay, but you feel the saliva pooling in your mouth, making you feel like Hooch.

Coughs escape your lips. Try to clear the throat. Hack hard into your lungs.

It feels like ice picks stabbing the lungs. Body doubles over. Barely able to catch breath.

Cough so hard tears stream. Dab at them. Put on a tough front,

A cancellation is maybe the lord's answer to prayer. Take the break. Head out the door.

2:02 am. November 22, 2019

2:38 a.m. November 23, 2019

I've been a bad girl again. I wasn't trying to pit one against the other. I didn't need to.

What the fuck was I thinking? Why would I want one to meet the other? It kinda worked.

When someone shows up on the door unexpectedly, it is easy to miss a few things. I probably should have tried to straighten up a bit more. I'm not known for being the world's best housekeeper.

When he asked me about the condom between the sheets that had been used by somebody else, I could have lied. I could have said it belonged to my brother, that he must've hooked up with some chick at the drum circle. I didn't really feel the need to lie, because I really didn't need to be dishonest.

Sometimes you have nothing to win, lose, or prove. There wasn't a reason to lie, as I felt justified. Why should I lie when I didn't feel as if I gave a fuck what he thought at that precise moment?

I was always told that honesty is the best policy. Throw all the cards on the table. Bring all the players to the table to duke it out if they have to, just to see what happens: tell one about the other and let them meet face to face, just in case they had questions or wanted to compare notes on how to make my pissy wet, which is one of those things I would encourage them to do, but does that make me a bad person?

One might not be happy the other is around. Tell the first that he found the condom, asked you, and you had a no-holds-barred confrontation about when the cats away, the mice will play. How long can one stay away, before someone swoops in to claim what you discarded all broken and chewed up?

If you are not there, not providing, and most importantly, if I told you that it was over, then where's the question? When I said choose your addiction or me, and you chose your addiction, you have nobody but yourself...

12:23 a.m. November 24, 2019

He wanted to be able to say that I cheated. I had to keep reminding him that I had been perfectly clear things were over when he left for his addiction. I could not let him guilt trip me is he feeling I was wrong.

Reminding him of the hurtful things he had said, I only had to remind of a couple key events, without having to totally rip the wound that had healed into the Band-Aid. Expose the raw ache just enough. When someone gets hurt, it does not make them overly receptive to wanna get hurt again.

"Why didn't you tell me? When were you going to tell me?" All valid questions.

There were times when I wanted to say something. I seriously contemplated saying things. The major hesitation was the fear that he could not stand to hear the reality, as I feared he would kill himself.

Samael believed in polyamorous love. He was the one who convinced me not to say anything. When I told him that I wanted to tell him, he had cold feet and said not to mention his name.

Maybe it was just testing the waters. The moment I heard that I was going to have a visitor, I asked Samael to stand up for me, to claim me as his own, but he disappeared. When I wanted him to be the man of the house, he went to somebody else's house instead, leaving me alone to welcome him.

At least I got the used rubber off the dresser. If I would have just noticed the one wrapped up in the sheets, that would have saved a little embarrassment. Hindsight is 2020 On those type of moments.

It wasn't until the proof was gumming to his hands that he asked me. Samael had the idea to bring him to the drum circle, as he had already planned on bringing one of his whores. It's always great to see a man near and dear to the heart to hang on someone in front of you, as if to further smear it in a bit.

There was no room for me to say anything about it though. I was there with someone else, and he was there was someone else. If you're partnered up for do-see-do, it does no good to complain about it.

Let the chips fall where they may. I feel hurt, he feels her, and the girl he's with doesn't even know that he's fucking me, too, as she thinks she's special. Samael and I don't say much to each other, only lock eyes and share momentary smirks, knowing we both had secrets; the only difference is I came clean about my secret and didn't try to deny it, being totally unapologetic about it, given some history.

Scorpio and her husband sniffs around. They claim that they follow the sound of the drums. They thought that the gathering was simply homeless people, and they wanted to feed pizza and vodka to the homeless people, as the wife's son had been homeless and had committed suicide only months before.

She beelines to me, trying to call her son out of the shadow realm and into the circle. In doing so, she keeps unraveling the string unknowingly. I try to warn her to stop, but she pulls the words out of me.

Truth spills out of my mouth like beautiful Verbal diarrhea and fireworks. Instead of judging, she offers advice by

detailing how she and her husband swing
with other couples, at parties, and even
with her living son, as they see him at
parties fucking more than a dozen broads
in a night like a sex soldier.

12:58 a.m. November 24, 2019

11:36 p.m. November 24, 2019

While you had your blinders on, concerned only about Samael, others started to appear out of the abyss seemingly, guys you had known for a long time and forgotten about since being on the island. Suddenly, your phone was ringing off the hook, and you were forced to admit there were others on the planet. Just as some make plans to come visit, one pops up that you hadn't thought about in years.

Basically appearing on the porch unexpectedly, you're forced to deal with him. He has nowhere else to go, no money to get there, as there's nothing around for miles thanks to your brother's paranoia. Though he had been known for being fucked up, with no money and not really much of a shopping choice, it's easy for him to be sober, which shocks the hell out of your mother, who knows him drunk.

At first mention of the situation, Samael first threatens to "just call the police to take care of it." Next thing you know, he's encouraging it, having you invite him to drum circle, where he shows up with another girl, half to play it off, and half to show you that he has had someone else in the background. The thing that bugs you the most about Samael is that he does not seem to value your individuality.

Whereas, you could go back to the comfy bedroom slippers of a former lover who already knows what you're worth, who stayed up countless nights dreaming about you, and who knows those little spots that get you going the most, spots that Samael was still getting to learn, as he's too selfish. While Samael knew how to play you like an instrument to bring you to orgasm, he didn't yet know all those favorite spots of yours, as he was more interested in teaching you how he liked things to be done. In contrast, a former lover that already knows the spots doesn't have to be schooled on how to do it.

Samael had a rough streak to him. Though he tried to say that he wasn't into BDSM, he sure has hell had a safe word, instructed you how to bite his dick and drag your teeth down his cock, all while digging your nails into his nutsack, not quite deep enough to draw blood from the family jewels though. At first, you felt uncomfortable with the biting and teeth dragging, thinking that it surely must hurt him, but he put his finger in your mouth to demonstrate exactly how he wanted the motion to be like on it.

Surely, he found a few of your spots from playing around, but he's not been observant enough to know which areas react when stimulated various different ways. Your former love already knows these things and doesn't require a roadmap to know how your body reacts to certain stimuli. Then again, Samael had some stimulation that not everyone contains in their bag of tricks, so to speak.

At first, your brain demand loyalty to only one person, and since the most recent person was Samael, your mind wants to be faithful, even while watching him hang all over another girl. Logical sense says fuck that shit. Logic says make your former lover prove his love through hard labor skills.

Stay means work, not play. There's got to be something done each day. Do a daily chore.

Earn to be kept, which will drip effect down to the sushi restaurant to it. Super rolling paper are now available at the circles for anyone who would rather have someone roll their own. Smoke 'em up.

12:12 a.m. November 25, 2019

12:29 a.m. November 25, 2019

She advises me not to feel guilty. Fuck whoever I want. Life is short.

She feels the connection between my former lover and I. She basically tells him to get over it. If you don't like the pussy that's on the menu, you can always move along on down the dusty trail elsewhere.

As much as I hate to see Samael leave with another gal, it's nice to be appreciated by someone who knows the pain of losing me and wants nothing more than to prove themselves worthy again. Come when called, go down when told, suck feet after being on them all day, run back, and clean the house. Samael was not the type known for moving and shaking in the cleaning department, but he's the type that would help if needed; he's more of the

type who expects the women to be to
pregnant wit a hut.

12:47 a.m. November 25, 2019

11:19 a.m. November 25, 2019

There's a different sexual connection
to someone who worships you, versus
someone who is just fucking you. The
electricity of a kiss can be felt pulsating
through the body. It's similar to the
electric connection of simple sex, as the
people try to substitute sex for love, but
the intensity is different; sure, there's a
climax in both cases, but the intensity can
vary with a simple touch or kiss, the
longing and need.

When the lips touch, it's either a
longing to explore every crevasse of the
other person, or it is simply a motherly
kiss like you'd give your grandma a peck. A
simple hello kiss, such as the French

greeting with a kiss on each cheek, varies greatly from a French kiss where the tongue is tasting what the other person has been tasting, whether it is food, wine, gum, or another person's orifice's flavitings of that day.

The French has a saying that translates to a man never looks behind the door, unless the man has stood there once before. With Samael, he has stood there so many times, he simply assumes there's permanently someone there, standing like a guard at work. He has intimacy issues getting too close.

11:34 a.m. November 25, 2019

1:23 a.m. November 26, 2019

The desire to please can be overwhelming. Striving to meet and exceed Samael's expectations makes me a better person. Yet, the lowered, nearly non-existent, expectations of an ex is even easier to exceed.

Lower standards equals less stress. There's something to be said about being chill, letting it all hang out. It beats having to walk on eggshells, worrying if things will be alright, even if he's lost on his phone.

On the other hand, it is nice to be pampered. Instead of having to please someone else, it's nice to simply lay back, relax, and let somebody else worry about pleasing you. As pleasing as it is to serve others, being able to make them happy, as you can make their lives easier, it is even more satisfying to sit back and let others prove themselves to you, trying to prove themselves as husband material.

Is it more satisfying to make dinner, or do you get just as much having dinner made for you? Is it more satisfying to clean the house, or is it more satisfying to come home to a clean house that has been made spic and span just to make you happy? Sometimes, it's nice to have over the reins, to be able two of us.

1:40 am November 26, 2019

The first chore for the former lover is to go down on you. It's not that you like to see the guy you were just trying to make a baby with leave with someone else, and you had to admit that oral sex was not his strong point, so you had to remember what it was like to have it from someone who knew how to do it exactly the way you like it. There's no instruction manual, pop quiz, or homework required.

There's no roadmap to the clit video needed, as he knows not only where to find it, but the best way to stimulate it to make you get wet on command. When he gets you close to orgasm, he plunges a couple of fingers inside with a come hither motion that taps the g-spot awake without even trying. Getting you off is so ingrained into him that it's become second nature, a pre-programmed setting.

Sure, Samael got you off, but he was more concerned about himself getting off than you. Thus, he wasn't attuned to what buttons of yours to press for immediate reaction. He had been starting to learn those spots and crevasses, but he got distracted when another vagina slapped him across the face.

So used to all or nothing mentality, you didn't want to settle for just part of Samael's heart. You didn't want to have to share his affections with others. It's easier to settle back into a throne that you'd previously abandoned to adventure onward to something exotic, only to get weary of travels and return.

Samael's younger at heart and maturity level. On other things, he was far superior, but loyalty was your biggest concern. You'd rather be worshipped and treated like a queen than rough it.

Even though your brother was into camping and paranoia adventures that involve prepping for the end of the world, just in case it should happen, didn't mean that's how you wanted to spend your time. His perspective got you to see that Samael was not as good as you thought he was, and Brutha reminded you that there was a lot of other fish in the sea who had previously been fawning for your attention and affections. Your brother would rather hang out with Samael, but he knew your ex wasn't over you, and he knew about the other guys around that had been vying for a scrap of your time.

The cop would randomly text you from time to time. There was a musician, and the financial attorney would send nude videos. It went from nothing and nobody to too many to choose from.

That's how your brother's perspective goes though. You had been guilty of making it that way, as you would randomly insist on him going on adventures, not telling him what kind of adventure he was heading into, simply telling him to hop in a car with you. Over the years, you'd gotten him into more than a few questionable times that went from not one person to a block party in the blink of an eye.

Your brother knew that you were not happy in a situation that was not monogamous, and he even tried to prove that it could be possible, but in trying to show that it could be possible, it only further exposed the truth of the jealousy and hurt feelings that come up with more than one person. Samael might be trying to fool himself that lust is all anyone needs to feel satisfied, but that's only because he has some intimacy issues where he doesn't trust himself getting too close to anyone. You cannot change if he's been hurt in the past, just as he cannot change your mind on polyamory.

You've been one of those people who is best with a partner to rely on, someone who is there through the thick and thin. Sex is not the biggest thing, as it ranks below loyalty and honesty. Not everyone has the same priorities you do, but you couldn't bring yourself to want to share with anyone.

That dirty love can be appealing. When somebody worships you so much that they don't care if you'd been in the shower or not, can look past whatever tattered garb you're wearing, and is willing to lick any of your body parts, no matter how sweaty or nasty, just to taste you. Going to the levels that others will not go to is what shows that true devotion to wanting to make things work out again.

Where did this old lover come from anyhow? You hadn't even remembered having a relationship with him, until he showed up at your front door. It'd been so long since you'd seen him, he was more like a stranger than a lover, and he had to remind you of the connection you had before.

Had Samael erased some of your memory? Did you get rid of other memories from being so focused on Samael? Either way, the more Samael stayed away, the closer you got to your ex.

1:11 a.m. November 27, 2019

12:42 a.m. November 28, 2019

Wanting to pick up where you'd left off as if nothing had happened, your ex could not understand what made you want to be done with him in the first place. As much as you wanted to give him the benefit of the doubt, there were little things from before that made you want to be done. Most of it revolved around his addiction, such as how violent he'd get, but if he's trying to be sober, part of you wanted to give him that chance, being very weary of when the other shoe would drop, of course.

Another part of you was broken. The battle scars had changed you, deformed you. Part of you felt like an old alley cat who had been through a lot of scraping, being left with an assortment of scars.

Some of those scars had gone to your heart. They say when a part of your heart dies that it does not regrow. There's definitely a part inside your heart that seems to have died a while back.

Part of you wanted to move on. Part of you wondered what if? Part of you was done caring.

When you got with Samael, it was too easy to move on and forget. Your ex had fallen off of your radar. The only reason he came back on was because he tracked you down and simply showed up.

Hard to tell people you are dead if they see you with their own eyes. Not that you owed him or anyone else any kind of explanation as to why you do whatever the hell you feel like doing. Still, if he's making the effort, why not indulge him a little bit, just to see if he is going to fuck up like people think?

Simply trying to stake a claim in your territory, he knows that you will not turn him away if he's sober. He knows that he oughtta be on his best behavior if he ever wants to have a last shot with you. Him staying away too long directly resulted in you hooking up with someone else after a couple years.

Still, it's the point that he did stay away that doesn't set well with you. He had chosen the lifestyle over you. He only strung you along, as you treated him better than his own family did.

Your mom would ask you, "do you want a boy? Or do you want a man?" She was right.

Simply showing up does not buy you a seat. You were keeping your options open now. Samael opened your eyes to the fact that others were interested, even if he was still interested in others.

There was police officer who would check in with you from time to time, just to see what was going on apparently, as the two of you never actually went out of any dates. Was he more interested in having someone to text once every couple of months? You'd hoped that he would have been manly.

The musician could play, but he didn't play with you very often, preferring the company of men while playing music, even though he had been in female-fronted bands before. This was a guy whose biggest fantasy involved a tranny: "somebody with big tits and a big cock would be the ultimate." There was something about knowing that his ultimate fantasy did not involve a girl that didn't set so well then.

He could totally come over, cook and clean for you, then worry about the other house afterwards. That's what some of these projects require: lack of sleep, and maximizing the hoppin, skipping, and jumping. Did your fantasy involve a guy catering to your whim to get stuff done?

1:09 a.m. November 28, 2019

11:51 p.m. July 28, 2022

Change perspective when the musician dies unexpectedly, as musicians often do. Sick of living life through your brother's perspective of being stuck out in the wilderness of no man's land, living as if technology had been forgotten about, it's almost as if you willed the game to change perspective to your mother's point of view, as she saw you as more of a princess. Her point of view was back similar to what it was like when you first arrived on the island, not having to choose to kill or be killed, but designing the island for the players who would be visiting the land.

You're above the stupid game. You're more than a designer of the background. You're the princess, as your mother would often introduce you.

"...And this is the Princess," she would gush. Often saying it with such enthusiasm, just to get whoever she was talking to in a rush to meet you, she was your best hype man, as she loved the "don't you know who I am?" game. It makes people wonder.

Are they supposed to know you?
Should they know you? They start to feel a
bit dumb not knowing.

Mommy said if you're the princess,
then some people are simply here to do
your bidding. You have always been good
at delegating. Do this, then that.

Of course, that means staying busy,
constantly rushing around, always
overseeing things, ordering people to order
things for you. It's fun, in a way, but it's
lonely in another, as you get too busy
staying busy. Connections do not fall by
the wayside, as you see people when you
want for what you want, but it's not the
same as when someone is your equal by
your side.

Everyone seems to want something
from you. Keep your friends close and
enemies closer, as you can never be sure of
the true intentions, guard always up. It's
great to be pampered, anything said goes,
but it's exhausting after a while as well,
and connections with people are fun but
fleeting, only sticking around when they
want something that you have to give
them.

Get bored and do silly stuff. Tranny action doesn't seem outlandish at all. Goose and gander.

Pretty soon, are you giving the island a run for its money, just out of sheer boredom when you're busy? Where's the crazy island creatures to spice things up a bit? Aren't they there for your disposal after all?

What can you get the demons to do for fun? How twisted will they let you push them just because? Are you going to start a war in your kingdom from being as curious as a cat and fucking around with demons, or are you smart enough to play with some other kind of creature from the island for safety?

12:11 a.m. July 29, 2022

10:31 a.m. July 30, 2022

The word safety flickered like an old light bulb. Inspiring a meditational moment, ponder the word. Safety has been an issue from the start, as people kept warning you that a demon will eventually hurt you.

Mom's perspective serves to protect. You knew that much, and if the game changes with perspective like you knew, and you were called here to design for some reason, then you should be able to design an out. Review what you know about the game, that you have to kill or be killed, but if you didn't make that choice...

What brought you here? Real estate, which is something that your mother taught you. Everything you know about real estate practically you learned through your mom, though you perfected the skills.

Your first step on the island seemed to be like a few lifetimes ago, as each perspective change seems as if you are shifting into a new life. Scenery shifts, as do the characters involved, but it's as if you had already been living the life fully up to the point where you remember it starting in the first place. It's like another dimension that had been simultaneously taking place, and you just happened to open your eyes.

Living through other people's perspectives, making your way through each, though it's familiar territory that you already seemed to know before arriving there, only gives you further insight into each. In their eyes, this is how things would take place. Not everyone sees things the same way, like alternate universes, slightly different story change with some similarities just to make it all the more confusing.

Something about real estate kept bugging you. What were you doing before you came on the island? Think back to what you had been doing directly prior.

Why were you coming up blank? You lived before being on the island. Why couldn't you remember anything before arriving on the island?

It was something to do with real estate. Had you been out showing houses? Were you holding an open house, or did you just sell a house of some sort?

You could picture putting your hand on a doorknob. Focus on the doorknob. Try to force your perspective back a few feet, and take in the doorknob.

Picture your hand reaching out to grab the doorknob, and you can see yourself grasp it and twist. Back up more. What's before you reach out for it?

See your hand open, as your arm reaches out. That's not back far enough. What do you see around?

It's like your vision is a tunnel, and the only thing you can see at the end is the door and the knob. How come you can't see the whole house or anything in the neighborhood? Why was your memory being blocked out, as if someone did not want you to remember anything that happened prior to being here?

Think. Focus on the door. No memories.

Grab the knob. Twist. Let the door open.

The door doesn't fully open. You twist, and you hear the latch click as if it will open, but it doesn't. As soon as you hear the latch, time freezes again, and your memory seems to blank out again with the door.

Samael enters your brain. Push him out. What's he have to do with anything involving the door?

The old lightbulb flickers. There was a connection between Samael and the door. For the life of you, the details seem to fall away from you though.

Focus on the light. Illuminate the doorway. What was it that you were trying to remember here?

Your mom's perspective wants to protect you. You can feel her desire to push you to remember. Deep breath, breathe it out slowly, and try to brighten the light to illuminate the doorway more, take in details.

Across the street. Picture yourself across the street. Try to be across from the doorway and look at it, so try to force your visual focus back from the door.

Why would you be across the street? How did you know there was a street there? Did you look across a street and see the door for the first time?

Picture boxes being moved through the door. Who went through that door? What were you seeing?

Surgery. The lightbulb flickered on for just a moment, something to do with surgery. Was it a hospital, or were you thinking of a doctor's office?

You knew it was something darker than that. It was not necessarily a place to help people at all. You knew that the door was not necessarily good news.

You knew you were across the street from the door at some point, and you had to try to focus on seeing a street in front of the door. Will it to come into focus. See the street, and see the building with the door on it, take in the details for a moment, focus.

Young and old, the doorway knew no age limits. Were you supposed to find this doorway as a way out? You knew it was more of a way in, but into where?

That was your way onto the island. The light flashed on. That was the door from the Murder House.

A flood of memories tidal wave over you, drowning you with the intense feelings of sorrow from all the people who fell victim to the Murder House. No, it was not the hospital at all, more of a makeshift black market surgery center for organs from victims. That door was merely a portal to this other dimension.

That bitch trapped you in here. That's how you were bouncing between perspectives, dodging demons. She thought she could spin the tables of time again.

Creating a black hole of sorts, the island was more like her creation, and while she let you design where you were trapped, she didn't have complete control, so she didn't really have a choice in the topic. Samael had a say, just as much as she did, but others did, too, as a portal is not owned by one individual. That's how the perspectives take control at times.

This was not the real world as people knew it. You had known that for a while, but you liked pretending. Reality is you're stuck in between worlds.

This limbo mocks reality, makes you think that it's real, but it's not. It's very far from anything real. Yet, it's more real, as it can spark the reality you feel.

That's great that you're finally figuring out where you are and all, but how the hell does that help you break out of it? Do you have to find the door, or do you have to find her? Is she even able to stop reality?

Where's Samael? He's with her. Of course.

That's why you had to keep locking up his dick. You knew that bitch was constantly trying to get it. He's not strong enough to resist that kind of lust, so he left, time and time again, just to make you miserable.

She wanted you to be miserable. She wanted you to know what it was like to be second choice. She wanted to create a reality with him in it for her only.

Was he even worth it? Nah, let the bitch have him. If he wants her so bad, let the two of them play.

Does he even know if he wants her, or is the reality she created simply convincing him he does? If he would waver here, he would waver anywhere. Scenery has been created, but it's individual choice.

Maybe they have a kid together here. Equal and opposite as before, different dynamics. Let them play house, and you're happy doing your own thing.

Great insight. How do you leave now? Time to go anywhere but trapped inside a Rubik's cube of dimensions, so how can you go about getting away?

Where's Adam these days? Could you distract her with a different penis? Let her be distracted by Samael's penis, as you try to tiptoe out of the scenery.

How can you get home? Where is home exactly? Where is it that you'd like to go to?

Feel the island begging for your perspective. Don't give into it. Don't start picturing where to go.

All you had to do was picture what you wanted. You knew how easy it would be to give in, but you didn't want to change the scenery just yet. You needed a plan, and you simply seem to keep coming up blank.

Should you picture the bitch with a spear in the middle of her chest? Would that help your cause? Think of the best plan of attack, then implement it.

You'd already tried caging up his cock and balls, and that sure as hell did not stop him from straying over to her. It's not like you would ever really be able to trust his ass, as he did wind up hurting you. As much as you hated to play second fiddle, you did not want to have to convince someone to love you.

If he has to be convinced, it's not true love. He's a demon with demonic tendencies that will only hurt you in the long run, no matter how you slice or dice it. At least Adam is not an angel, and not like he's the only man left on earth or anything, but it's the point.

In your perspective, you can have an army of naked men catering to you if you'd so choose. You can have naked women doing sexy stunts from the ceiling, aerial delights. All you have to do is picture it.

Why is the concept of love so important with Samael in particular? Why not anyone else? If she wants him, and he wants her, then why fight them?

That's what she wants. She wants you to forget him. Thing is, he already seemed to have forgotten you a while ago, so it seems as if her agenda won.

Chalk it up as a loss. What did you really lose? A demon will always wind up hurting you in the end.

Sometimes, you have to cut your demons loose. Let a demon go be a demon and do demonic stuff. Can you change someone's true nature by sheer will?

11:31 a.m. July 30, 2022

11:36 p.m. July 30, 2022

Busy yourself by building up your fortress. You know that you will need it. Thing about being royalty is that everyone is out to try to steal from your kingdom.

Everyone likes to see a ruler fall. You cannot be weak, so you have to try to build yourself up to be as strong as you can. Anticipate the attack before it comes.

You can let the two love birds live happily ever after, but that won't stop it. That's just one side of the illusion. The defenses must be built in times of peace.

It's like being trapped in a pyramid. You think you see things clearly, but that's just one side of many that look flat. Refractions of light happen to create illusion, making you think you see rainbows of shimmering pretty colors.

Look past the illusion. Look through it. See what is being obscured behind it.

Maybe you should go after her. Romantically speaking. Maybe you should try to seduce her away and show her how much better off you are being on your own.

The best defense is a good offense. Don't give any of the boys a second thought. Come into your own on your own.

Don't wait for the shining armor that has not seen the dings from any battle. That does not speak of experience in life. One that is battle hardened and jaded is not always so great either, as it always seems to turn into another one that is ultimately seeking a nurse or a purse.

You can chase after a man through a million different scenarios, or you can stop chasing and find the happiness inside yourself while building up your defenses. It's not time to get soft and fat, but it's time to trim up and firm up the loose parts. Get yourself battle ready, while others are comfortably getting lazier.

Growing independent from being let down is not the worst thing you can do. Fix your own problems, and don't rely on all the smoke and mirrors and promises from all of these guys with big talk. If you cannot fix it yourself, call the expert, and not just some average Joe who will say that you used him and now you owe him.

While you want to hate her, you really feel bad for her, as you know he's controlling her the same way he did you. That's why part of you wants to save her. Confront her and the controlling situation.

Show her there's more to life than that. Do you really want her to know that though? Maybe you want her to stay miserable with him, so you can be free.

With his mind tied up in her, it allows your mind to be free about everything. It's not like you were obsessed over finding another guy, as you were finally fed up with all of them. When you stop struggling and fixating on some guy coming to whisk you off your feet, you can finally enjoy simply being in your chosen surroundings and change it if you want to.

Go on nightly rounds to see around the crevasses of your kingdom. Try to learn every nook and cranny. Spot when things look out of the ordinary right away.

You notice more when you're not distracted by trying to watch some guy. Learn the routines of those around you. Don't let them realize that you know.

Habits are so ingrained, people do not even realize that they have them. It's so second nature, the routine runs so deep. Creatures seemingly run on autopilot.

Visit all the areas of your kingdom. Know it in and out. Then get shocked.

What's this? What are all these bodies? They seem to be hooked up.

The bodies do not move, but they are not dead either. They have wires connected to their temples. Images display in their minds like as if on movie screens.

They see what they are programmed to see. Are each of them seeing the same? It seems like multiple are on the same loop, but not all of them are being tuned to the same programming at the same time.

Do you know them? Do you see familiar faces? Do you just want to believe that you see familiar faces out of loneliness, just to say you know someone?

It's all part of the game. These are players. They're killers and victims.

12:06 a.m. July 31, 2022

12:51 a.m. August 1, 2022

Thick fog floats around you. How did you even find this place? Where was this massive holding tank, and just how many players were there connected at once?

Squint closer. Gasp. It's you.

It's her, too. It's him. All of you.

The child was connected, too. The idea of a child flickered somewhere in the back of your head, but the concept almost seemed foreign to you now. How long has it been since you've seen children playing?

How long have you been here? How long have you been connected and limp? That can't be good for the muscle mass.

You thought about calling out to her before, but you felt like you needed to now. You didn't even have to say her name aloud, just think it, and she will appear. Lilith, you might want to check this out.

She was next to you, just the two of you, and she was none too thrilled to see you. Before she can begin a rant, you're your eyes, shake your head no, and hold up one finger to indicate that she needs to shut the fuck up and be quiet a second.

Point that finger that you are holding up towards the pile of bodies, and direct her eyes to look with your eyes at her body.

"What the fuck are you showing me?" She took a step backwards. "Is that me?"

"You didn't know this was all part of a game? You thought it was happily ever after? How happy was it after all for you?"

She stares at you blankly. For once, she doesn't know what to say and does not know whether she should really hate you. Something in the center of her was thawing, melting like ice in the hot sun.

"Why didn't you call him?" She looked at you in disbelief. "Why me?"

"Maybe I was sick of his bullshit. Maybe I thought we were not really meant to fight over his stupid ass, because you're one of the realist chicks I know, one of my true equals. If we're both trapped, in this together, I didn't want you to think I was reaching out to him, as it's not about him."

Suck saliva down your throat and grit your teeth, before you continue. "It's about us. Is there even a jealous love triangle, or is that to fuel us to keep playing this game without realizing?"

Rubbing her chin, she arches an eyebrow. "How do I know this isn't a trap? How am I able to trust you, out of anyone?"

"Bitch, you don't have to trust me," you snarl at her, "but don't you think it's a little odd that our bodies are on either side of his, one body apart from each other, and you don't seem to remember playing? Tell me, when did you sign up to play exactly? Did you choose to kill or to be killed?"

"I never made that kind of choice," she stammered. "I never signed up to play a game," she insisted. "He came to me."

"Do you remember the house that I lived across from? Do you remember the murder house where they chopped up bodies for the black market organ business? Do you remember the kid?"

"I see the kid," she stared. "That's his kid, but is that my kid or your kid? I honestly do not even remember anymore."

"Then it's time to stop the game." Stare into her eyes. "We need to put this behind up, whatever it is, and focus on us."

"Shouldn't we get him? What if he knows the way out of here. He can help."

Shake your head and insist, "he doesn't know the way out of here, or else he wouldn't be hooked up there with us. He's not going to help us right now. He will only divide us, and we can't have that at the moment, not until we know more."

She knows you're right. She also knows there's no plan. It's great that the two of you have joined forces, and maybe he could help, but not quite yet at least.

"Lilith, who would be able to contain the three of us, and not only the three of us, but so many others more? Who would be able to hook us up to a machine like that, and neither of us have any knowledge of it? How do we not remember, and why are we at each other's throats if we are in such close proximity in peaceful slumber?"

She did not have any words. "By the way," you continue, "I met this dude named Adam. He's with this chick Eve."

Her eyes flashed red. Shake your head at her. "What are we all doing here?"

1:21 a.m. August 1, 2022

2:27 a.m. August 2, 2022

"Tell me honestly," you squint at her, "did you have anything to do with this? Do you know anything about how we got here? Where's the furthest back you remember?"

"Would I be looking over my body in confusion if I had something to do with this? This is the first I am seeing this, so I do not know how it came to be like this. I know our house here, and I remember a house before we moved into this one…"

"How much do you remember of that house? Where's the kid if not with you or I? Do you remember any kids lately?"

She shook her head no. "The last time I recall seeing a kid was at the other house, and that house didn't have a lot of children's stuff that I recall in it either. I'm not sure what I remember, as I try to recollect what the furnishings look like, it continually fails me, my memory fools me."

"Like someone has purposely blocked parts of both of our memories, you mean?" Watch the words sink in. "If you don't think that you're here for any part of a game, not as a player, and not as a designer, then why do you think that you are here, a part of this, or did you think it to be real, like a part of reality in real life?”

“He loves me,” she stammered. “That’s real,” she tried to convince herself. “We have a house here, a life here…”

“Uh, and how normal is that life?” Arch an eyebrow at her quizzically. “Do you have friends over for tea and crumpets, discuss local politics and sales?”

“Sounds like Adam and Eve had a strange sort of normal. I’m not one to judge. You remember Adam at all?”

“That subservient slut deserves his ass,” she snarled. “Glad he found someone to stand beneath him. Yeah, I know him.”

“So, what you’re saying is that you’re a little used to being controlled, so Samael doesn’t even seem that bad, huh? His lil temper tantrums seem legit, eh? How many times has he stepped out on you?”

She fumed silently. Shake your head at her. “I’m not here to accuse anyone of anything, but why don’t either of us remember having a kid, and is that ours?”

Her eyes darted up and to the right. The information was downloading, casting a shadow of reasonable doubt onto all of it. "Who would want to put us into a portal, wipe our memories, and change perspectives of scenarios, forcing us to see through other people's eyes at times?"

"Is the question who or why? What purpose does it serve?" Stare at each other in the eyes without blinking, think.

2:51 a.m. August 2, 2022

1:31 a.m. August 3, 2022

"Speaking of who," she cocked her head to the side at you, "I cannot even remember your name. I know that sounds bad, but I just remember that I don't like you. It's like I don't even know why I don't like you, especially since Samael does tend to whore off, trying to knock up bitches, so it's not like it's your fault he's like that."

"My name is not important," you pacify her for a moment, skip around the question, as you don't want any bad memories to come rushing back too fast. "Honestly, I'm over him whoring around, too, so if you want to put up with it, cool, have his warring ass, but I'm just trying to figure out what's up with our bodies there. It's like I'm trying to come in peace or whatever, as this is bigger than our dislike for each other if we are trapped together."

Point down to the limp bodies. "We do not seem to be warring with each other or anyone laying nearby each other. That's why I wanted to take the guy factor out of the equation and talk to you woman to woman about this, no jealousy for now."

"I can," she sighed, "I can put my feelings aside when I know it's to protect myself from whatever may come across me laying there hooked up to whatever it is." It seemed like the harder the two of you tried to look at the setup, the hazier it got. "It's like I keep having to strain to see it, but for some reason I know Cain is the child, Samael's bloodline in the garden."

"Who is the mother? Are you the mother? He's close by you, not next to."

She snarled. "Eve is the mother." She shook her head, "Adam thought that child was his, that Eve was all his, but no."

"Adam doesn't know?" You looked at her in disbelief. "He thinks that's his son?"

"Lil halfbreed killed his real son," she laughed. "That's what started the line of the giants, but they've bred their way back to normal size, a defense mechanism to fit in, evolution over the years. They just say that humans used to be smaller back in the day from the lack of nutrition, but they just needed a few years of giants to breed."

"Lilith, how do you put up with the killing? I mean, I know it's part of his job and all, but how do you put up with the random bodies and wild times around?" Shake your head and sigh, "it gets to be too much for me at times, like I want to have a companion and all, but when it involves that level of shit on an everyday basis, it's like I really didn't have a partner around."

"It gets lonely," she agreed, "but I bide by time joining in on some of the fun. I shouldn't admit that a part of me likes it, but I do like to tag along from time to time. It would be nice to take a break from some of it, granted, I get what you're saying, but I guess I always accepted that was part of the deal if you want to have him around."

"I kind of reached that point where it's sort of nice not having all that around. I missed it at first, felt like I was isolated in the middle of nowhere, but the killing still followed, like I'd wake up in the midst of it, not knowing when it started or why. It's not like it was killing for fun, as there was always a reason why, it was justified and all, but it's like it gets old after a bit."

She nodded, "I can understand where you are coming from for sure. I've been dealing with him for centuries now, and we've had our run-ins, our ups and downs.

God knows, he loves fornicating with humans, and it's gotten him in trouble."

"Like I said," clear your throat, "let's just take him out of the equation for a while. Let's talk about what we know about why we are here in the first place and how the hell we can escape safely. Do we even need to escape, or are we paying extra for those hookup services there?"

1:59 a.m. August 3, 2022

11:01 p.m. August 5, 2022

"Lilith, it might as well be the first few of us and all of our descendants that are hooked up to this machine of being. It's like we're trapped in this pyramid, bouncing in and out of this game of life. Do we really die, or is it just a new life?"

She looked you in the eyes, confused. Your words were sinking in like information downloading on a computer, and it takes a moment to process all of it. Her blank look was all the response that she could muster at the moment.

"Is this just a glance at the souls? Are we really just the same souls that are being reincarnated, starting new lives like starting a new video game as a new character? Is this game just life, however we make it, no matter how many times and ways we mess up, and we are simply supposed to keep trying to learn from it?"

"I've always known," she finally said, "that if I didn't like the direction I was going, I could simply change it, right or wrong, simple as that, deciding to change. I have killed you off a few times, and you have killed me, as I can feel it in the deepest part of my being, but here we are. How are we still standing here, yet still lying there, unless we have to progress?”

“Reach nirvana. Turn life into how you want it. Give the Angel of Death an entire island to claim souls on in an infinite number, just keep bringing them back in a new form, a new storyline.”

Touch her face with your hand. “We have always have the power to change the storyline. I’ve decided that I’m sick of his shit, and when I put my mind to change it out, others came to me, whether I wanted them to or not, like lost puppies following.”

Inch closer to her face. “Sometimes, I get fed up with the idea of men all together. That’s when I wonder why we would fight, petty jealousy over a penis, when we have so much more to offer than what others want to acknowledge from us.”

You thought she was going to take a step back, but she only moved closer to you, her hand now touching your face, too. “There’s a fine line between love and hate.” She reached in to kiss you deeply, her hand moving up and into your hair, nails parting strands of hair ever so gently.

Sometimes, you don't need a man to feel fully satisfied, and there was something much more pleasing about intimacy than trying to kill each other. Centuries of hate in a moment turn to lust. Pull each other closer and feel as if the world is being sucked into a void with you.

It's the perspective changing. Scenery brightens up. Sky turns rosy.

Was it sunset or sunrise? Did it matter? Time suspended as hate melted away like a glacier in the sun, slowly fueling the burning lust of passion more.

Sucked into the wormhole while sucking face, it could be seconds, days, weeks, or centuries passing you by. Time didn't matter, only the sensation of her. Body against body, feeling the perfect curves of each other, honoring and respecting an equal that knew the basics of how to treat the other, something that the guys seemed to have forgotten about.

How had you shared Samael and Adam, but not shared each other yet? It's like you've been a half step away from each other the whole time, at each other's throats in the wrong way, as you should have been gently kissing and sucking that throat the way you are now, feeling her pleasing you back in a way you denied yourself for centuries – or had you? Was this the welcome embrace from too long of not touching each other, or the first time?

Whatever it was, it felt right. It felt way more comfortable than any of the guys. It's like the two of you had been purposely separated by guys, just so they could all have their way with you, before the two of you could finally find each other.

Being trapped on the island, really hooked up to this machine of life, the two of you were only one body away from each other, so even if you hated each other, you were still closely bonded to each other, like it or not, regardless of how or why, you were always only a body away from each other, like they had to keep you away from being able to touch each other, as they knew the two of you would be too distract to do whatever it was they wanted you to do. What was is they really wanted you to do anyways? Maybe they wanted you to figure out after a few too many centuries that the two of you were really lesbians?

Maybe this pyramid is nothing more than a cardboard box with a dead cat in it? Anything is possible, until you open the box. The cat could be tap dancing, you don't know, until you open the box and see.

11:33 p.m. August 5, 2022

She kissed your nose and smiled smugly, "I was wondering how long it would take you to come to the other side. You were tempted by a serpent all right, more of my sloppy seconds, and how was Samael compared to Adam exactly? More of the same as we all know, because the names change, but the game is the same."

Your jaw drops. "You?" Tilt your head at her inquisitively and squint.

"They got their spawn out of you. Good thing they didn't have DNA tests for when that serpent-like penis entered you. Cain keeps the knowledge of the garden, because Samael was not kicked out, only you and Adam, as you chose to pretend like it was Adam's, being a piece of his, insisting, and how did that wind up?"

The hazy fog was lifting from your mind, as it was rushing back to you now. "You know how that ended," shake your head. "Able started with an A, like Adam."

"They're no different from tom cats," Lilith cooed. "They'll kill off another's offspring to ensure the longevity of their own line. They only wanted us to breed."

She ran her fingers through your hair and whispered, "when was the last time you had romantic intimacy without them trying to plant a seed in you? Why do you think you cannot lock up Samael's penis? They're programmed to impregnate, and they only look at us as breeding material, then move on like it's another run of the mill day, not caring about what you get up to after that, as they know they have trapped you."

"Is that why there are no kids?" You thought she didn't want you distracted by the responsibility of breeding, like it's the right thing to do, keep pumping them out. "I thought I was coming to you on my own, but this whole time, you were waiting?"

"It has to be your own decision," she kissed your forehead. "We don't have to stay trapped in the perspective of what other people think is right or thinks that we have to do. We have the power to change things and make it the way we want it, so we don't have to stay on the island of perpetual death, just because that's what Samael wants, ya know?"

She motions over to the sea of bodies, but the two of them were some of the only women visible. Looking closely, it was mostly men, some boys, but mostly men. "They're hooked up to their own fantasy, full of testosterone and death, and while some might claim that we might have more testosterone than the average female, that does not mean we have to travel in the seas of testosterone when we have the ability to fly off with our own estrogen."

Blink. Head tilt. "Fly off?"

"Who said we have to stay here? Is there a law forbidding us from going back into our bodies? As long as we don't disturb the others, we should be fine."

Was she crazy? Was it that simple? Will yourself back into your body, and just try to silently unplug from the masses?

She nodded her head yes, as if she could read your mind. "Ready?" She bit her lips and raised her eyebrows at you.

One small nod. She smiles. Go.

Close your eyes. Will yourself to go back into your body. Feel chains breaking.

Take a few deep breaths, before opening your eyes. Wires are connected. Reach up to the back of your neck, pull the plug out of the base of your head, and the disconnection makes a sharp breath.

Try not to scream. Bite your lip. Only a breath can be risked at a time like this, as you didn't know what all this male energy might do to a girl like you now.

Yank the port out of the inside of your elbow. Another unexpected inhale. It hurt a lot more than you remembered any hospital visit trip taking out a blood line.

Take three deep breaths and try to steady yourself to move upwards and out. The weight of gravity felt heavier than normal, as if your muscles had atrophied. Limbs like heavy lead weights, try your best to wiggle them awake and get the blood flowing, moving fingers and toes.

When you try to put weight on your feet, you nearly let out a groan, but caught yourself, looking around to make sure nobody was making their way towards you. Lilith was not moving yet, but you could not let that concern you, as it was fight or flight time to simply get the fuck up and out, regardless of who is going with you. Trying to stand, ankles and knees crack so loudly, you get paranoid someone heard.

Shift your eyes around all directions. Was that a cough? Turn your head around and notice that Lilith is staring at you.

Extend a hand. She grabs it. Help her stand up and unplug from the men.

Grasp arms, using each other to balance, tiptoeing between the menfolk, trying your best not to wake any of them. To your surprise, they were all into the frequencies, not wanting to break away. Lilith can tell the expression on your face, and she simply shrugs her shoulders, motioning for you to come on, like there was nothing for either of your there now.

None of the men even seemed to notice the two of you leaving, so wrapped up in their own fantasies of how life should be according to their own mind's view. It was almost too easy for the two of you to sneak out of there with little incidence to report, simply making your way to the nearest exit and back out into the world. Neither of you could recall how you got entangled into that mix, but you were both more than ready to leave, all too eager to create your own perspective together.

When you reach the door, you and Lilith both put your hands on the knob at the same time and turn it together. When you walk out, you see your apartment across the street. You were simply walking out of the murder house, only this time, you had a friend to bring home.

Nod up at her. Smile. She smiles back, as you step out of the door together.

11:57 p.m. August 6, 2022

More by Marisa

Marisa L. Williams earned her Master's in Writing at the Johns Hopkins University and her Bachelor of Science at the University of Toledo.

She is a licensed real estate agent in Michigan and Florida, as well as a professor and the author of more than 100 independent books.

For more by Marisa, visit www.outlandishwriter.com, www.lulu.com/spotlight/thorisaz, follow her on Twitter @Booksnbling or on Instagram @Thorisaz.